PRAISE FOR AURELIS AWARD—WINNING AUTHOR SALLY ODGERS!

BOY UP TOP

The light grew, and then two shafts of gold shot down like spotlights.

"They call it the Eyes of God."

I felt a long shiver go down my back when Patrick said that.

"Patrick..." I said.

"Yes?" His arms tightened around me and I felt him kiss my cheek.

"You're not...an angel, are you?"

There was a silence, while Patrick watched the sunrise and I waited for him to answer. Then the sun came up in a hard rim of gold like a giant's collar, and I saw the landscape spread below us, green as emeralds. I think I gasped, because the landscape really was below...hundreds of feet below.

We were sitting in the clouds.

BOY DOWN UNDER

UNDER

B 5185 0416601 2

Sally Odgers

SMOOCH NEW YORK

For Darrel, James and Tegan.

SMOOCH ®

October 2004

Published by

Dorchester Publishing Co., Inc.
200 Madison Avenue
New York, NY 10016

ISBN 0-8439-5453-1

The name "SMOOCH" and its logo are trademarks of Dorchester Publishing Co., Inc.

Printed in the United States of America.

Visit us on the web at www.smoochya.com.

BOY DOWN UNDER

RASPBERRY JELL-O.

Ro to Mahalia Thomas. Ro to Mahalia—come in, Mahalia! Call me, Hallie. Write me. Send me an e-mail. Do something to let me know I'm not in the twilight zone!

I squinch my eyes shut and send Hallie a mental message, just like we agreed. *Call Ro. Call Ro. Call Ro.*

And does she call? My best friend since our diaper days? Does she sense my misery and come rescue me?

Not a chance. Zip. *Nada.* Zilch. Not a whisper. Not so much as a tremble in cyberspace or a quiver in the ether.

Thanks a lot, Hallie. I owe you. Not. Don't forget some of this is down to you.

I open my eyes again. I look about. Same old, same old. I sigh. *Get over it, already! So you're stuck in a village at the butt of the world. It could be worse.* (So I tell myself.) You might be hiking through a tick-infested jungle. *You might be stuck in summer school. You might be flipping burgers at Greedy Gus.* I crank another sigh. I could go for a burger or a chili dog right now. I could swallow any diet buster with a thick

1

shake chaser. Gaining a few pounds then losing them again would give me something to do. Something aside from fret about the boy I met down under.

Boys, who needs them? I used to say to Hallie.

And Hallie'd give me the big eye roll and tell me, *We do, Ro! What's up with you?*

"Hey, honey." Mom's voice breaks in on my thoughts. Mom's smile pours over me, sweet and slow as molasses. Mom's as happy as a honeybee tucked up in clover. All her spiky edges have smoothed right down. She loves it here in Tasmania.

"It's so quiet," she says.

And I say she's not wrong about that.

"It's peaceful," she says. Just the place to do some work on her book.

"Don't you miss anything in Sydney?" I ask.

Mom shakes her head no. "What's to miss? Lectures, teachers, people, problems . . ."

"Listen up, Mom," I said, the first time she mentioned the P-word. (The P-for-peaceful, that is.) "You might find it peaceful now, but surely after a while you'll miss *something.*"

"What do you miss, honey?" asks Mom, gazing dreamily into the clouds.

And then in a rush I decide to tell Mom all about it. It can hardly matter now. . . . "I miss P—"

My voice breaks off at that point. Just snaps off like a rotten old twig.

"Miss what, honey?" asks Mom.

"I miss P—" My voice does it again. I struggle. I really do. I open my mouth and wrap my tongue around the words I mean to say. It's like talking through a mouthful of raspberry Jell-O.

". . . miss . . . ?" Mom actually takes off her shades and turns to stare at me. "You miss *what,* honey?"

"I miss P . . . *people,*" I say, lamely.

That wasn't what I wanted to say, but it's all my mouth can manage.

What I *meant* to say was that I miss Patrick. I wanted to say I miss Patrick Carroll with an ache that calm Tasmania can't soothe.

There! I said it. I thought it, anyway. If I close my eyes again, maybe I can bring him into focus. Maybe I can pin him to the sky like a butterfly on a board, like a shimmering mirage.

Ro to Patrick. Ro to Patrick. Come in, Patrick Carroll. Come back from wherever you went so we can fight some more.

The sky is the blue of the dress Mom wore to the prom a million years ago. There's a wisp of cloud like the stole she had over her shoulders.

And Patrick isn't there. Not on the clouds, not in the sky, not standing in front of me gripping my hands as if he'd drown without me. Not laughing and giving me the kiss-that-didn't-miss and saying, *Love, you, Ro.*

"Patrick," I whisper. "Oh, Patrick. Please come back."

"What's that, honey?"

Patrick.

The word never leaves my mouth. I try to mention him to Mom. I struggle to say the name. It's raspberry Jell-O time again. And now it isn't fair. Now that he's gone, why shouldn't I say his name?

"Ro, are you all right?"

"Yes," I say, but it's a lie. "Just a tickle in my throat."

"Fix yourself some juice," suggests Mom.

3

But drinking juice won't fix what's wrong with me.

"Patrick." It comes as the tiniest whisper. Mom doesn't lift her head.

"But, *Mom,* since when were you going down under?" (That was me talking, back in early December.)

"Hey, honey . . ." Mom's sweet, slow smile came out to play. "Since Dr. Craig's pickup had a fight with that semi. That's since when."

"But you can't go to Australia instead of Dr. Craig!"

"Why not? Wilf says we can take over the apartment Dr. Craig was planning to rent."

Wilf! I thought darkly. What sort of man calls himself *Wilf* these days? The name sounds like he should be a hundred years old, but Wilf Porchetto is no more than thirty. Wilf is Mom's agent as well as Dr. Craig's, and he's so sharp he'll cut himself one day on his own clever notions.

"Haven't the down-underites got their own educationalist behaviorists?" I asked. An educationalist behaviorist is what Mom is. Don't ask me exactly what she does. And don't ask me why I'm not a straight-A student. You know what they say about shoemakers' children never having shoes.

"Guess not, honey."

"Of course they have," I said sharply. "And they hired Dr. Craig, not you."

"That's right, honey, but I'm just as qualified." Mom shrugged. "I know this is kind of sudden, and if you don't want to come I'll understand. You could stay with your aunt Vida, honey."

And share a room with Doughy Chloe? Listen to her

4

wheeze the night away because she can't stay away from Dunkin' Donuts?

"I'll stay with Hallie," I said.

Mom frowned just a little. I saw the squinch between her eyes. "Not in a two room apartment, honey. If you come with me, you can do a year of high school in Australia. Their school year starts around late January."

I sucked my lip, thinking about that. Go to high school away across the world, thousands of miles from all the kids I'd known since elementary school? I'd gone through junior high with them—Beth Anne, Hallie, Josh and Alex, Shonee, Tav, and Tedson Wallace the Third. There were others too, but those were the ones that mattered.

"What do you say?" asked Mom. "It'll be an experience."

"Why not?"

Mom smiled lazily.

I'd already put in a couple months at Woodbrock Senior High, and it wasn't much different from the junior campus. I thought a school down under would make a change.

I was right.

"What about you and Alex?" my best friend, Hallie, wanted to know. "And what about *me-eee?* I'll be all alone."

"As if," I said. "You'll have . . ." I paused; then we both chanted, "Beth Anne and Josh and Alex, Shonee, Tav, and Tedson Wallace the Third."

Hallie rolled her eyes around in her head, like peeled black grapes. "They're not my best bud. And little old Tedson still isn't speaking to me. And what about you and Alex?"

5

"What *about* me and Alex? There is no 'me and Alex.'"

"He's got the biggest crush on you." Hallie stretched her hands out wide.

I pushed my bangs out of my eyes with both hands, and wished I could push the red out of my cheeks. "Where did that come from?"

Hallie looked me straight in the eyes. "Would I lie to you?"

What Hallie said weirded me out. Alex is a computer nerd, with zits. (Why do nerds have zits?) But he's kind of cute. His mom says Alex would never date a girl without a built-in modem. Guess his mom is wrong, if Hallie is right.

Hallie grinned, flashing her retainers at me. "You're blushing," she crowed. "Rowena Maven's *blush*ing!"

I put my hands over my cheeks. "It's because I'm mad. No fair," I added. "You can blush and who'd know?"

Hallie punched the air. "Black *rules!* You ought to see his screen saver."

"Why?"

"What would you care?"

By now I was getting mad. I thought she was winding me up because I was going down under and leaving her behind in little old Woodbrock.

"I don't care," I said coldly. "You brought the subject up, if you recall."

"He's got that picture of you from the junior high yearbook," said Hallie. "It's set to come up after an idle ten seconds." She grinned. "Guess he leaves it idle quite a lot."

6

"The one of you and me eating cotton candy? Yech!"

"I'm not in it anymore." Hallie turned down her mouth. "He scanned me out. And guess what he scanned in where I used to be?"

I didn't guess, so Hallie told me anyway.

"A little old candy heart."

"Yech!" I said.

"Hey, forget it. I bet you'll meet some cute guys in Australia." Hallie winked. "Pack your bikini, Ro."

"It's forty degrees," I pointed out. "I'd have goose bumps on my goose bumps."

"Australia's hot, and it's full of hunks. They all swim laps before breakfast, and they've got bodies to die for. You see it on TV."

I tossed my head to show I wasn't interested in bodies to die for. But still, I packed my bikini. I might have goose bumps that had just gotten past a training bra, but heat makes things grow, right? A year in the tropics and my lemons might be melons.

Dream on, Ro, I thought.

Hallie called me that night. "Hey."

"Hey, yourself," I said. I was still kind of sore at her.

"I'll call you," said Hallie.

"You just did."

"When you're in Australia. I'll call you. If my mom will let me."

"Telepathy's cheaper," I said. (I'd seen Mom's telephone bill after she'd been putting calls through to Australia.)

"You telepath me, then," ordered Hallie. "Every single day."

7

"Every single day," I agreed. "I'll send you a mental message." I hummed a spooky tune down the telephone.

"You'd better," said Hallie. She put on a voice like Ms. Fellows at school. "You must make an effort, Rowena, if you expect results!"

I laughed. Hallie always cracks me up when she isn't driving me insane. "Sure!" I promised. "I'll send you mental messages. You better answer, Mahalia Thomas."

"I'll do better than that," said Hallie. "I'll get Mom to enter those TravelSure promotions and win us a little old trip to Australia."

We laughed about that. Hallie's mom is a whiz at competitions. She clips coupons. She writes slogans. She's a genius with twenty-five words. She and Hallie joke about it, but the spooky thing is, she quite often wins! That's how she came to be doing a Pilates class while Hallie and I talked on the phone. She won a contest sponsored by some fitness magazine. They loved her essay on stretching and strengthening to reach new heights.

Getting ready to leave was kind of unreal. Mom saw to all the visas and paperwork, and Wilf kept calling and sending her more contacts, brochures, and bookings. Mom seems slow and sweet and lazy when she's in Mom mode, but when she steps into Dr. Marina Maven mode she kicks butt. It's like she becomes this totally other person, three inches taller and ten pounds lighter.

I used to think Mom was the only one who did the chameleon trick. That was before I met Patrick Carroll.

2

BOY ON A BALCONY.

The airplane touched down at Sydney Airport right after the New Year. It was seventy-five degrees when we left the airport, double what it was at home.

I felt like dissolving into a grease puddle on the sidewalk.

"Yech!" I moaned. There was way too much concrete, too many cars with sun bouncing off their hoods and rebounding off of my eyeballs. They all drove on the wrong side of the road.

"Come on, honey," Mom said. "Let's go crash in our apartment, and tomorrow we'll see the sights."

It wasn't as simple as that.

First we had to wait for our baggage. We'd traveled light, but we had to clear customs, and they practically took Mom's baggage apart. There were cute little sniffer dogs, but it was Mom's notebook computer and briefcase that caused the delay. Every pocket and zip had to be checked. I expected Mom to jump into Dr. Maven mode and rip into them, but she didn't.

"It's too hot for that, honey," she said. "Besides, they've got a job to do."

We took a cab to the apartment. It was not in the middle of Sydney. It was tucked away in a grungy suburb right out in the boonies. Way cool. Not.

"Can't we stay in a motel?" I asked as we drove farther from the heart of things.

"No," said Mom. "The apartment's ready. I figure we'll settle in better if we have our own things around us."

That was a joke. We never even unpacked.

We drove past little houses my Grandpa Maven calls "ticky tackies."

"Housing estate," said the cabdriver. He was driving with his elbow out the window. He took corners so fast I felt sick to my stomach. I closed my eyes until we lurched to a stop. The driver pulled our cases out of the trunk, swung them onto the sidewalk, told us to have a nice day, and drove off.

"Is *this* it?" I stared at the bleak apartment block. It looked way too old.

"Well, honey," said Mom doubtfully. She pushed up her shades to look at our new home. "It's different."

It was different, all right.

"Not what I imagined," said Mom.

It was not what anyone would want to imagine.

The real estate agent gave us the key, then showed us up the stairs. There was no elevator. No security grille. The air-conditioning was on the fritz. There were cockroaches lurking in corners. It was grim. It was the Roach Hotel.

Mom and I stayed in that apartment for three days. Every morning we caught a cab to the station, took the train into Sydney, and went sightseeing. We checked out the famous bridge, and the Opera House. We went to the aquarium and watched sharks swimming over our heads. We took a cruise around the harbor. We shopped at discount stores and ate out a lot. It was weird to see McDonald's and Burger King (only they call it "Hungry Jack's") like we have at home. Even the script was the same. "You want fries with that?" and "Have a nice day."

We did whatever we could to stay away from the apartment.

On the third day, Mom cooked oven fries for dinner while I fixed a salad. The smoke from the oven would have set off every smoke detector in the block, if they'd had batteries.

Mom had called the Realtor and said we needed somewhere else to live.

"Not a chance," said the Realtor. I could hear his flat Aussie twang over the telephone.

"We need to rent someplace else," repeated Mom.

The agent laughed. "In your dreams, lady. This is the high season."

Calling Mom "lady" is a big mistake. She snapped into Dr. Maven mode and chewed the agent out over the phone. "I wouldn't keep hogs in this apartment," she said. "Although it looks like someone else has been! Do you have the number for Public Health and Safety? And for the exterminator?"

"You don't want that, lady."

"*You* do," said Mom. "There are roaches. Tomorrow they get fumigated. After we move out."

"Move where? I told you—"

"Into the new apartment *you* are going to find us,"

11

said Mom. "Or would you rather call my agent in the States and have *him* explain how it's done? If you recall, you let him think *this* was a suitable place."

The Realtor said he'd let us know. He wasn't laughing anymore.

"Good one, Mom," I said when she thumbed off her cell phone. "Great for intercontinental relationships."

Mom pointed with her toe to the corner, where a big black bug lay with its legs in the air. "*That* is not great for intercontinental relationships, Rowena," she said. You note that she did *not* call me "honey." Mom "honeys" people when she's in Mom mode. When she's in Dr. Maven mode, the honey's thin on the whole-wheat toast.

The kitchen still smelled of old grease and smoke, so I walked outside to grab some fresh air. On the balcony, there was room for one dusty potted fern (dead) and one Rowena Maven, standing squished up in the corner. There was no room for anything else bigger than a cat. That's what I thought then.

I didn't look at the floor, in case I noticed cracks. I didn't touch the railing, either. I'd done that. Once. It felt as if it might snap off like a fry that's been left too long in the warming oven. It scared me, how brittle it felt.

I stared into the westering sunlight and watched cars zoom by on the wrong side of the road. I felt empty, bored, and uneasy. I wanted out. I wanted Woodbrock and Hallie.

Hallie would have laughed at the roaches. We could have gone walking and poked fun at the "balcony apartments" and checked out the cute boys down under. Not that I'd seen many so far. I never saw a blond surfer near the Roach Hotel. I supposed the cute ones were all at Bondi Beach on the other side of the city.

Australia was no fun on my own.

I wanted to go home.

Ro to Mahalia Thomas. Ro to Hallie—come in, Hallie! Call me, Hallie! Write me. Send me an e-mail. Do something to let me know I'm not in total Dullsville!

I sent my mental message halfway around the world. I pictured it streaking over the Pacific Ocean, closing in on the continental USA. I saw it zero in on Woodbrock like a rocket. Up the avenue it zipped to the John Stephen Apartments where Hallie lives. I steered my message to the elevator and pushed the button with my mental finger.

Ping!

The message zipped into the elevator, rode up three stories, then scooted through the door of the Thomas apartment.

Hallie was watching television, dipping into a bucket of popcorn, and scraping bits of kernel out of her retainers with one fingernail. The message hit her between the eyes and soaked into her brain.

Ro to Mahalia Thomas. Ro to Hallie—come in, Hallie!

Call me!

But Hallie just dipped back into the popcorn bucket. Some friend.

I blinked and shivered, then made myself smile. Hallie was miles away, and she probably wasn't eating popcorn or watching television. I counted back fifteen hours, the way Mom had told me. It was two o'clock in the morning, back home.

13

Two o'clock in the morning? Of course she wouldn't call!

"OK, *friend,*" I growled under my breath. I sent another message to the John Stephen Apartments. This time I pictured the night. I skipped the elevator, and sent the message in through the window, through the security grille, to plop onto Hallie's pillow. It started to ooze toward her sleeping face.

Yech! I shivered hard. This mental message routine was creeping me out. I flicked the message away from Hallie as if it were a bug.

"Goose walk over your grave, Rowena?"

It wasn't Hallie. How could it be? Hallie was far away.

Besides, this voice was male.

I snapped my head sideways. I *knew* I was alone on the balcony. There wasn't room for anyone except for me and the plant.

"Up here, Rowena," said the voice, and something bounced at my feet.

I squealed with shock. Don't ask me what I thought it was. It was too small for a grenade or a bomb, and it wasn't the right color for a firecracker.

"You jerk!" I hissed. "I nearly fell over the railing!"

"No, you didn't, Rowena. It's too high for that. It's only a tennis ball, anyway."

I craned my neck, but the balcony overhang was in my way. Whoever it was must be standing up there. I wished I hadn't called him a jerk. The next thing he dropped might be a brick.

"Up here," he said again, and then he dropped a little pink feather. I picked it out of the air and it gleamed in the sunlight. What kind of bird had pink feathers?

"Galahs do," said the voice.

"Say what?"

"The feather, Rowena. It's from a galah."

"Right." I didn't understand. I didn't know who he was. I didn't know zip. Then something hit me. "How did you know my name?"

"You told me. You're Rowena Maven. Ro."

"I did not."

"Didn't you?" He sounded really puzzled. "I must have heard it somewhere."

"I guess maybe you heard Mom talking to me," I suggested.

"I guess maybe," he mocked.

I waited for him to say something else. It was weird talking to someone I couldn't see. His voice sounded young, but you never know with guys.

"I'm not much older than you."

Lucky guess, I thought, and peered up again.

"Stay right there, Rowena." The boy dropped past and landed neatly on the balcony.

3

WALKING WEST.

I shied, nearly hitting my head on the wall of the apartment. I expected Mom to come rushing out. If she was still in Dr. Marina Maven mode, I expected she'd kick the boy back up where he'd come from.

No Mom.

The boy was in front of me, smiling. I'd thought there was no room here, but the boy stood between the plant and me. For a moment we were practically nose-to-nose; then he picked up the pot. He looked kind of astonished; then he turned and held it over the rail, opened his hands, and let it fall.

"Oops," he said.

"Is that all you can say?" My voice sounded scratchy with shock.

He cocked his head. "It seemed appropriate."

"You . . . you—"

"Jerk?" he suggested.

I felt myself blushing. "I shouldn't have called you that."

"Why not?" The boy grinned. "I've been called worse things, Rowena, I'm sure."

16

"Why doesn't that surprise me?"

"Don't be like that." He held out a hand. "Hi. I'm Patrick Carroll."

Bemused, I put my hand in his. I hadn't shaken hands with anyone since my junior high graduation.

Patrick's hand was warm and firm, not like the sweaty paws most boys have. He gave my hand a little squeeze then let go.

"W-well," I said.

"You bet," said Patrick Carroll. He looked me over, as if I were a species new to science. "You're American," he remarked.

I shrugged. "You're not." I'd known that right away. I supposed he was Australian, but he didn't have much of an accent.

He was taller than me, probably around six feet, and I figured he weighed about one hundred sixty pounds. He was wearing blue jeans, a plain white tee, and running shoes, and he looked about sixteen. Maybe seventeen. I inspected his chin. No zits, but he'd started shaving. He was cute, but not to die for. He'd have made maybe a six on Hallie's hunk-o-meter.

"Seen enough?" He hitched one eyebrow toward his buzz-cut hair.

"Too much," I said. I stared at his white T-shirt. It was as clean as a laundry advertisement. "What are you doing here, Patrick?"

"I'm talking to you."

Wise guy, I thought. "I mean, what are you doing here on our porch?"

"I'm talking to you," he said again. "You want to go somewhere else?"

I almost told him to get lost, but I was kind of

curious. "You live up there?" I pointed with my thumb.

"You live down here?"

"Not for long," I said. "Mom's called the Realtor and told him to find us someplace else." I paused. "There are major roaches."

Patrick held up his thumb and finger, two inches apart.

"Not quite that major," I admitted.

"They are up there." He jabbed his thumb upward, the way I had before. "Getting on for armadillos." He looked at me hard. "You need beautiful places, Rowena. Want me to see about that?"

I laughed. "Sure. I guess." As if! If Patrick knew somewhere nicer, he'd be there himself, right?

"Come for a walk, Rowena?"

I guess I should have said no, but there was still daylight left, and I didn't want to stand on the balcony for the next hour. "Maybe," I said.

"That a yes or a no?"

"Guess it's a yes." I turned to go back through the door and into the apartment. "You'd better hold your breath as we go through," I warned. "The oven caught fire an hour ago."

"I'll meet you down in the foyer," said Patrick.

I tugged the balcony door open and ducked through. "Sure," I said, "but you'll have to come through this way unless..." I didn't finish the sentence, because Patrick wasn't there.

I went back onto the balcony and leaned gingerly over the rail. No Patrick. I peeked down. Not even a stain on the sidewalk. I twisted my head to look up, but no way could he have climbed back past the overhang. Had he rappelled down? Sprouted wings? I looked for a fire escape or a hidden ledge. I gave up and went into the apartment. Maybe he slipped behind and past me as I turned?

"Mom?"

"Not now, Rowena." Mom had her cell phone clamped to her ear. She was tapping her toe. Someone had put her on hold.

No "honey" for me. Mom was still in Dr. Maven mode.

"I'm going for a walk," I said.

Mom flapped her hand.

"I'll be back soon."

"OK, but don't get— Yes?" Mom's attention snapped back to the call. "Of course I'm still here."

I went into the poky little washroom and stared at my face in the spotty mirror. My mouth drooped and my bangs lay limp across my forehead. I picked up a comb, then tossed it aside. Patrick Carroll probably wouldn't show.

I walked slowly down the steps. I didn't want to get there too soon, in case I was disappointed. I hate to be disappointed, so sometimes I try not to look forward to things in case they turn out wrong.

Patrick was waiting in the foyer.

He smiled. "Are you ready?"

"Sure." I stepped past him onto the sidewalk and blinked as the sunlight dazzled my eyes. "Which way do we go?"

"Whichever way you choose," said Patrick.

I looked up and down the street, but neither way looked attractive. "You choose," I said. "Is there someplace pretty?"

Patrick seemed to consider. "We'll go west," he decided.

"West?" I'd been thinking more about left or right, but I *had* heard something on the radio about the western suburbs. "OK," I said, "but not too far. I told Mom I wouldn't be more than half an hour." That wasn't what I'd told Mom, but I wanted an out if Patrick wasn't as nice as he seemed.

"We'll be back before she notices you've gone," said Patrick.

" 'Zat so?" I thought he was joking. Then.

I walked with Patrick down the patchy sidewalk, watching where I put my feet. He didn't ask what grade I was in, or the names of my favorite bands. He asked weird stuff, like what kind of animal I was most like, and how I'd choose to spend a perfect day.

"What about you?" I asked. "What animal are *you* like, Patrick?"

"A chameleon, I think."

"A chameleon. Right. One of those lizards with eyes that track like gun turrets."

"They blend into any background. Now you see it . . . now you don't."

"And that's you?"

"Oh, yes," he said thoughtfully. "I'm an expert at blending in, Rowena. And at not being noticed."

"*I* noticed you," I pointed out.

"That's because *I* noticed *you*."

"Why did you?" I really wanted to know. It's not like I'm a babe or anything.

I didn't expect flattery and I didn't get it.

"You looked out of place."

Well—duh!

20

I'd been watching my feet take steps along the sidewalk, avoiding the cracks so as not to break my mother's back, as the saying predicted, avoiding lumps of gum that had gone hard and shiny in the sun. Now I tried to picture Patrick in a different background. Not this grungy suburban backwater, but somewhere more romantic. The problem was, I couldn't recall what he looked like. Were his eyes blue or brown? I remembered he was tall, but was he sturdy or slim? Was his skin pale, or freckled, swarthy, or even black?

What was it with this guy that I couldn't even recall if he was African American or not? I'd always thought I was a pretty observant person.

I peeked at him. He had pale skin, blue eyes, and light brown hair, cut short. He was cute, but not to die for. About a six on Hallie's hunk-o-meter. I'd come to that conclusion before, I recalled, and I wondered how it had slipped my mind.

He turned his head and smiled. "There are more important things than appearances, Ro."

I smiled too, then looked back at my feet. . . . "Yech!" I said, and scraped some gum off of my shoe on a patch of dirt.

I'd taken another five or six steps before what I was seeing snapped into focus. I stopped dead, like I'd banged into a wall. I'd been on the sidewalk, but now I was standing in a garden. "Huh?" I said. "What's with all the flowers?"

"Pretty enough for you?" Patrick sounded like he'd planted them himself.

What? I sneaked a peek to my left and right. Flowers and more flowers spread in a carpet around us.

I turned slowly through 180 degrees. I was standing

on rich brown earth, and all around me, dotted thickly, were clumps of flowers. They were yellow and orange and flame-colored, and standing out among them were pea-shaped flowers that were scarlet and black. They didn't look real.

"They *can't* be here," I said. I squinted at Patrick. "*We* can't be here."

"Why not, Rowena?"

"They just can't be, is all." I looked around again, turning on my heel. My chin started to wobble. "Or I can't be. Or something. We were just on the sidewalk and now we're not." I knew I was babbling, so I swallowed and took a deep breath. "Where are we? How did we get here?"

Patrick touched me lightly on the shoulder. "These are the wildflower meadows. You wanted somewhere pretty, so I walked you here."

"This is a park, right?"

Yeah, right. A park we'd stepped into while I wasn't watching? A park that stretched as far as every horizon? I twitched away as if his touch had burned me.

"It's the wildflower meadows," said Patrick again.

"Yes. Right." I was feeling a little sick to my stomach. I knelt down among the flowers, and put my head on my legs. I could smell green growing things and I could feel the crumbly texture of the earth. *In a moment,* I thought vaguely, *I'm going to be freaking out. I'm going to start screaming.*

"Don't you like it, Rowena?" Now Patrick sounded like a guy whose girlfriend had thrown a candy heart back in his face, or laughed at a poem he wrote her.

I took more deep breaths, and noticed the perfume

growing stronger in the air. It was sweet and fresh, and smelled nothing like the flowers in a florist's store.

I don't believe this. This is wild.

"I-I . . ." I stammered. There seemed to be a lump of clay in my throat. "I g-guess we should be getting back." I clenched my nails against my palms. "C-can we go back?"

"We only just got here," said Patrick. "I was going to take you for a walk in the clouds, but we can go back whenever you want. Are you OK?"

"I guess." A shrub of yellow flowers brushed against my cheek. "*How* do we get back?"

"The same way we came," said Patrick. "Sure you want to go?"

"You better believe it." My hands were damp and my knees felt like cotton candy. Patrick tried to help me up, but I didn't want him to touch me. I was way scared.

I meant to watch carefully as we went back (if we *could* go back), but Patrick distracted me with conversation. I was watching . . . watching. The flowers still spread around us, and whenever one brushed my leg I felt the touch. The black and red ones looked kind of like plastic or wax.

I tried to look for the city, but my attention kept catching on little things, like red flowers and butterflies and the little smudged line on Patrick Carroll's cheek. I blinked when I noticed that. It hadn't been there before.

I was dragging my attention back to the horizon when a big old wind blew up behind me. For maybe two seconds I saw the flowers shaking on their bushes, and then my hair flew right up and flopped over my face. When I clawed it away from my eyes, I was back on the sidewalk, maybe fifty feet away from the apartment block.

I almost burned rubber as I made for the Roach Hotel. I ran like an ax murderer was after me, instead of . . . well, instead of Patrick Carroll.

I hammered on the door until Mom let me in, and then I collapsed, panting, in one of the hard chairs. I didn't even check for roaches before I hit the seat. My heart was thudding like a gong and black dots danced in front of my eyes.

"What is it, honey?" Mom was in Mom mode again. "Where have you been?"

"I've been—" My mouth framed the words—*I've been out with a boy called Patrick Carroll, and it was wild*—but nothing came out but the first two words.

I strained my ears for the sound of Patrick's footsteps. I felt like I'd wandered into a slasher movie.

"Never mind, honey," said Mom. "I've just this second gotten off of the phone to the Realtor. Guess what? He's found us a place we can move into tomorrow. It's near your new school." She smiled at me. "Does your mom kick butt, or what?"

- 4 -

AWAY FROM THE ROACH HOTEL.

"Mom, something really . . ." My voice thinned out like stretched gum. I couldn't say the words in my head. You know those DVDs where someone has something important to say and nobody listens? You feel like yelling, *Just spit it out, already!*

It was like that. I tried to tell Mom what happened, but the words were dammed inside my head. Mom didn't seem to notice.

Then something got through my panic.

"We move out of here *tomorrow?* We can leave the Roach Hotel and move into a proper apartment?" I said. "Great! The sooner I get out of here the sooner I get away from—" This time my voice snapped off like a piece of elastic. I almost heard the twang.

Patrick Carroll, said my voice inside my head. *The sooner I get away from Patrick Carroll.*

"You'd better believe it, honey. Pack your bag," said Mom.

I hadn't unpacked, but I went into the rank little bedroom and closed the door.

Then I came out and locked the door onto the balcony.

The potted plant was back.

I didn't sleep well that night, and it wasn't skittering roaches that kept me awake. In my mind, I saw flowers. I heard Patrick Carroll's voice, disappointed because I didn't like his surprise.

I liked it, I said inside my head. *It just wasn't right. It wasn't really there. I wasn't really there. It was impossible!*

My mind jerked away from impossible, and I tried to think of something else. I pushed my mind back to the aquarium. Mom and I had walked down the zigzag concrete paths and under the big curved tanks. Big old sharks had swum over our heads, so we could look up and see their jagged teeth. Sharks have cold eyes.

Thinking about sharks made me shiver. It kept my mind off of Patrick Carroll.

Bright and early we left the Roach Hotel and caught a train to Clancy, on the North Shore line. I expected another apartment block, but our new home was a regular house.

"Good, huh, honey?" said Mom.

"How did you get ahold of this?" I asked. "Didn't the Realtor say there was nothing on the books?"

Mom grinned. "It belongs to some guy Wilf knows. He's out of the city a lot."

"How come we're renting it?"

Mom shrugged. "Listen up, honey, don't look a gift horse in the mouth. There's a student who usually caretakes, but she's going to her mom's."

Mom looked to be walking on air instead of on a sidewalk.

It was a one-story house, so no strange boys could drop from the balcony. I was thinking that when the student met us at the door. She was dressed in a retro seventies print and she looked kind of like a girl from an old painting. "Dr. Maven? And Rowena?"

Mom and I nodded.

"I'm Sorrel Rose," she said. "I'll show you round, but there isn't much to do, apart from the birds. I expect Mr. Porch—"

"Much to do?" echoed Mom.

"Didn't the estate agent tell you?"

"You mean the Realtor?" I suggested.

"Do I? Probably."

"He didn't tell us a thing until I got the thumbscrews out," said Mom.

Sorrel's lips shaped a word you don't say aloud to strangers, and then she sighed. "Dr. Maven, I hope you don't mind birds?"

"Birds?" said Mom.

"It would be great if you'd feed the owner's birds while you're here." She shooed us down the path as she spoke. "It's just a couple of galahs. Their aviary has a seed hopper and self-watering—"

"*What* did you say they were?" I broke in.

"Galahs," said Sorrel.

I peered into the cage. The birds were kind of like parrots, but I hadn't seen parrots that color. They were gray on the back, with really bright pink chests and little frills of feathers on their heads. They had eyes like orange beads. "Galahs," I said.

27

Galahs. Pink feathers. A pink feather drifting through the air.

The feather, Rowena. It's from a galah, said Patrick Carroll's voice in my head.

Galahs.

I licked my lips. "Are galahs, like, rare?"

"No, no! Lots of people keep them as pets."

"They're cute, aren't they, honey?" said Mom.

I nodded. If galahs were common, that meant Patrick Carroll had nothing to do with this place. Probably. I gulped in a deep breath.

"You just need to refill their hopper every week, and check on their water," said Sorrel. "You can give them carrots and things, too. The keys are on a Peg-Board in the kitchen, and there's a list of useful numbers above the desk." Sorrel took a card out of her pocket and gave it to Mom. "Here's my mobile number, in case you want anything. I can come back if you need to be away overnight."

After Sorrel had gone, Mom and I unpacked.

"All this, for about what we were paying for the Roach Hotel!" gloated Mom. "Unbelievable, isn't it, honey?"

Unbelievable. Words echoed inside my head, and this time they weren't mine.

You need beautiful places, Rowena. Want me to see about that?

Patrick had said that, I remembered. And I had (kind of) agreed.

I tried to keep my eyes from bugging. Then I gave myself a pep talk. *Coincidence,* I told myself. *Impossible,* I told myself. *Wilf arranged it,* I told myself. And, *Whaddaya think this Patrick Carroll is, then, Ro, some kind of wizard?*

As if. A wizard in a crummy apartment block.

So forget about it, already! I instructed myself. *If he drops in again, tell him to go fly a kite!*

The house was neat. It was way better than the Roach Hotel, except for one thing.

It was every bit as lonesome.

On Monday, Mom started work. She had, like, twenty lectures and meetings to do in the first month. "You'd better come with me, Rowena," she said. "See a little of the socioeducational environment."

Uh-oh. Mom was back in Dr. Maven mode again.

I tagged along on the first three jobs, but then I rebelled. When I was younger, I used to think it was neat to have a mom addressing meetings and crowds of teachers, but it's no fun now. This is the scenario.

Mom—no, make that Dr. Maven—and I arrive at the venue.

Mom introduces herself and me. People nod hello, and then basically ignore me. Now and then someone asks me questions. Like, How old are you, Rowena? Like, Isn't it neat to have a mom like yours, Rosina? Like, I trust you're a straight-A student, Joanna?

I don't like being ignored or being grilled and having people get my name wrong. It's insulting.

"Hurry up, Rowena," said Mom on day four.

"No, thanks, Mom. I'll chill out here for the day."

"I'll be gone until four," warned Mom.

"I'll just hang out at the park. I might meet some of the local kids."

Mom tossed her hair. "Fine. But call me at noon. And if anything happens—"

"I'll call Sorrel," I said. "Nothing will happen. Stop stressing, Mom."

"Call me," said Mom. "Or else."

Mom headed off for Clancy Station, and I chilled out. I turned on the radio and got a traffic report.

I turned on the TV and got a ticker-tape parade of daytime soaps and talk shows. One channel was showing American infomercials. After the seventh invitation to "Call now!" I locked up, pulled my light sweater on over my capri pants, and started walking.

There was nothing happening in Clancy Park, apart from a bunch of little kids in the playground. I walked around the little trails and looked at little gardens with labels fixed to them: THE FERNERY, PEONY PATCH, WILDFLOWER CORNER.

There were butterflies flipping about, like living barrettes. I heard a chattering, squealing noise in the trees above. I looked up and saw what looked like a bunch of kids' umbrellas hanging in the branches. Bats!

I motored out from under there before one of them pooped on me.

I sat on a wooden seat by the Fernery to catch my breath. It was ten o'clock, and the day stretched like an empty road. Where did the cool kids hang out in Clancy? *Not* at Clancy Park.

I counted back fifteen hours, closed my eyes, and tuned in to Hallie.

It was seven P.M. on Wednesday in the John Stephen Apartments, so Hallie would be doing homework at the table by the window.

I put my fingers against my temples and sent her a message.

Ro to Mahalia Thomas. Come in, Mahalia! Send me a mental message.

I pictured the message arrowing in on Hallie. I saw her jump and blink, and then a big bright Hallie special spread over her face. Her mouthful of metal glittered.

Hey, Ro! What's going down in the Roach Hotel?

We moved out into a regular house in Clancy.

Way cool!

Way not.

How's the land down under, Ro? Met any hunks?

Only one, and he's weird.

Hey, yeah?

He—

Hallie put her finger to her lips and rolled her eyes left and right.

Gotta go, Ro. Call me!

Ms. Thomas popped her head in. *Mahalia Aretha Thomas! Have you finished that math?*

I blinked and came back to earth. For a few moments there I'd felt like I was really talking to Hallie. I closed my eyes.

When I look again, I told myself, *I'll really be there. I'll be sitting over from Hallie doing math with her. One, two, three—open your eyes! Tah-dah!*

I opened my eyes.

Tah-dah!

"Hello, Rowena."

I wasn't in the John Stephen Apartments. I was still in Clancy Park, near the Fernery.

Sharing my seat was Patrick Carroll, the Wizard of Roach Hotel.

31

- 5 -
"TRUST ME."

I shied like a startled colt, and scrambled away. I could feel my eyes bugging.

"It's you!"

Good one, Ro. How lame is that?

Patrick smiled. "You bet! Aren't you pleased to see me?"

"What are you doing here?" I spluttered. I was so lonely I would have been pleased to see Count Dracula, fangs and all, but I didn't tell *him* that.

He cocked his head. "Haven't we had this conversation before?"

"Very funny." I eyeballed him, taking my time. He looked the same way he had at the Roach Hotel. He had on basic blue jeans, and a white T-shirt that looked like it cost maybe five dollars at Wal-Mart. White sneakers, designer—not. Who wears stuff like that to impress a girl? Therefore, it was obvious that Patrick Carroll was *not* out to impress Rowena Maven.

So what did he want?

"You look as if you'd seen a ghost," said Patrick.

I blinked a few times.

Have I seen a ghost?

I didn't say it out loud. It was such a dumb idea. He looked kind of wholesome, like the boy next door.

"You're a long way from the Roach Hotel," he said.

"So are you," I pointed out. I swiveled my eyes about.

Kids in the playground. *Check.*

Moms pushing baby buggies along the path to the Peony Patch. *Check.*

Some guy setting up a soft serve stand. *Check.*

There were plenty of people around if I hollered for help.

"I won't hurt you," said Patrick.

"Darn right you won't," I said. "Where did that come from?"

"You don't seem pleased to see me. Your eyes are sort of . . ." He swiveled his eyes left, then right, without moving his head. "I'll go away if you want." His mouth turned down like a sad clown's, and he made puppy-dog eyes.

"I'm thinking. I'm thinking." I bit the inside of my cheek to keep from smiling.

What would I do if he went? Go on sitting by the Fernery until I got moss on me? Go join the moms and their kids at the Peony Patch? Buy a soft serve, and have it melt all over my sweater? And if he went, how could I be sure he wasn't making like a stalker behind the Wildflower Corner?

"You can tell me to go anytime," said Patrick.

Darn right I can. Darn right I will, if I want to.

"Come for a walk?" Patrick gave me the puppy-dog look again.

"Where to? Not west. Uh-uh."

"What about the beach?"

"Bondi Beach?" I felt a stir of interest. Hallie had promised blond surfer boys at Bondi. "That'd be neat," I said. "I guess there are phone booths there?" Call me Miss Goody Two-shoes, but Mom would ground me for a month if I didn't call.

Patrick got up. "You'll be back in time to phone your mother. Cross my heart."

"That's OK, then," I said. "Guess you've got a heart to cross?"

"Oh, I have a heart, Rowena. Sometimes I wish I hadn't." He walked a few steps and turned down one of the twisty paths between the little gardens.

I was about to follow when I hit rewind in my head, and replayed what we'd said.

Me: I guess there are phone booths there?
Patrick: You'll be back in time to phone your mother.

"How did you know I had to call Mom?" I blurted.

"You told me."

"I did not."

"You must have." He turned around, and we eyeballed each another. Time seemed to stretch like bubble gum; then Patrick's face relaxed. "You asked if there were phone boxes, remember? 'Phone booths,' you said."

"So?"

"So you're planning to phone—I mean, *call* your mother. Obviously."

"How is that obvious?" I gave him a look straight

34

out of the Dr. Maven handbook. The *don't mess with the Mavens* look.

Patrick tried a shot of puppy-dog innocence. "You got a lot of friends in Sydney?"

"Well . . . no."

"There you are, then," he said. "It had to be your mother. Don't worry, Rowena. I'll bring you back in plenty of time."

There was still something out of kilter, but I wanted to be convinced. I wanted to walk on the beach with this boy down under. I wanted some fun.

I followed Patrick down the twisty path. "How's the Roach Hotel?" I asked. I lengthened my stride so I could walk beside him, and almost ran into a big old shrub that was blocking a lot of the trail. I couldn't avoid it without bumping Patrick, and girls that bump guys are, like, so *obvious.* I pushed my way through the springy branches.

I smelled a sweet, peppery scent from the yellow flowers on the shrub, and then I smelled the clean, salt breath of the ocean.

There was loose sand under my feet. It sifted into my flip-flops, and I heard the *schuff-schuff* sound of it as I walked.

"What do you think?" asked Patrick.

He was standing a little way off. There was a strong breeze molding the white T-shirt against his body, and the racing cloud shadows were playing peekaboo across his face.

Hunk alert, said Hallie's voice in my head.

Don't be dumb, I said back. *Hunks don't wear plain white tees.*

So? Why are you grabbing an eyeful?

I peeled my eyes off of Patrick. Then I noticed something.

"You jerk! You did it to me again!" If he'd been closer I would have popped him one on the chin.

"Did what, Rowena?" Patrick gave me double-barreled baby blues, but I didn't buy that puppy-dog look this time. I know about puppy dogs. Puppy dogs chew your Nikes and spit out the eyelets.

"As if you didn't know! You've brought me to . . . to . . ." I frowned. "Somewhere else," I said. It sounded lame, but what else was I going to say?

"I said we were going to the beach," said Patrick.

"This is not Bondi!"

"Forty miles of white sand to ourselves. How's that a bad thing, Rowena?"

"But—"

But . . . *You don't find gorgeous beaches like this with no one on them!*

But . . . *You don't find places like this a few steps from the city!*

But . . . *This isn't happening! It can't be true!*

My heart stopped trying to climb out my mouth and settled where it belonged. I *knew* this wasn't possible.

It wasn't happening, and yet it was. And *that* meant Patrick Carroll was some kind of magician.

That should have weirded me out, but I was just a bit ticked off. "*I* get it," I said to Patrick. "You've hypnotized me, right? And when you count backward from ten we'll be back in little old Clancy Park."

Patrick gave me a sudden, wicked grin, and I pictured Hallie's hunk-o-meter ringing all the bells. My stomach rocked and rolled.

36

"Want to start counting now, to test that theory?"

Did I? My tongue kind of froze to my palate.

"Trust me, Rowena. I won't let anything hurt you while you're with me."

It was kind of cute, the way he said that, but kind of sappy, too. *Trust me?* When a boy says that, you watch your back. The boys you can trust would never say *trust me.*

My tongue came loose and I gave him the slow hand clap. "My hero."

The grin faded to a cute half smile. "Is that what you want me to be?"

"Who needs heroes, hero? I can look after myself." I tried to see the park, but the endless sands covered it completely. "What is this place you've magicked up?" I asked.

"It's Ocean Beach," said Patrick. "Out there's the Indian Ocean." He pointed out at the long waves rolling in. They *looked* real, but I knew better now.

"Says you," I muttered. "What's really out there?"

"Africa," said Patrick. "Eventually."

"Oh," I said. Little old Woodbrock is tucked away in a valley, and the ocean's a five-hour car ride away. I see it maybe three times a year, and it doesn't look like *this.*

I pulled my gaze away from that misty horizon, then followed Patrick to the ribbed edge of the ocean. I hunkered down and dabbled my fingers in the froth of a wave. It was cold, and it felt the way water ought to feel.

This must be kind of like virtual reality.

Patrick took his running shoes off, and I stole a peek at his feet. Hallie says you can tell a lot about a boy from his feet. There was this guy she thought was a real hunk, until she saw his knobby toes with long black hairs on top. She went right off of him.

Gorilla toes—hello? she said when she told me all about it.

"No gorilla toes here," I said. I clapped my hand over my mouth.

Good one, Ro. How lame is that?

Patrick tied the laces of his running shoes together and held out his hand for my flip-flops. "I'll put them up by the path with mine."

I kicked off my flip-flops. My ears were burning, but I rolled up my pants legs and dabbled my feet in the waves while I waited for Patrick. The cold salt sting of the water almost had me convinced the place was real.

"So," said Patrick, making me jump. "You think I'm a jerk, but you reckon my toes are hot."

Before I could answer (as if I could have thought of one thing to say), he splashed off along the edges of the waves. I trailed after. *How lame am I?* I kept thinking, then I thought, *What does it matter? I'm not really here, so I probably didn't say what I thought I said, and maybe Patrick isn't really here either.* Hello? *You're out on the sand with the wizard of the Roach Hotel?*

I felt way better after that.

We walked for miles. The wind kept whipping my bangs about, but it wasn't wild enough to blow sand into my face. Sand in the nostrils is not a good look, even in virtual reality. I picked up a piece of driftwood, polished silver-gray by the wind and sand. It felt kind of smooth and cool.

It's not real, I reminded myself, but the sand swished between my toes and the wind off of the ocean chilled my cheeks. Gulls were screaming overhead, and there were birds leaving pockmarks in the sand.

"Those are terns," said Patrick. He paused. "That's why they're taking turns to leave tracks."

I groaned. "That's really lame, Patrick. That's *so* eighth grade." I looked back toward the trees. High dunes humped up toward the sky, and there was a kind of ripple of long grass. It looked like fur on a Persian cat. "What's up there?"

Patrick didn't answer. I turned on the spot like a music-box dancer. He wasn't anywhere.

"Ten, nine, eight," I counted aloud. "Seven, six, five." I paused hopefully.

Come on, Patrick. Come back! Tell me to stop the countdown!

"Four, three, two—" I stopped. I guess I was scared to go on.

"Patrick?" I said. Then I hollered, "Patrick Carroll, you get your butt back here!"

"I am here, Rowena."

His hand on my shoulder made me whoop with surprise. "Patrick, you—" Rage blocked my throat so I couldn't finish what I meant to say. Patrick finished it for me.

"Jerk?" he suggested. "What have I done this time?"

"You disappeared, then sneaked up behind me!" I growled. "You are so dead if you do that again!" The back of my neck felt spooked.

Patrick looked puzzled. "I've been here all along."

"You—" I broke off again. *Had* he been there? If I *could* see sand and dunes and ocean that I *knew* weren't really there, why shouldn't I fail to see Patrick, even if he *was* really there?

Maybe none of it was there.

"Forget it," I said. "What's up behind the dunes?"

"Come and see! There's an awesome view from the clouds."

I laughed. "You can't get that high, Patrick."

"Want to bet?" Patrick made a run at the long slope of sand and rough grass. I followed, keeping my eyes fixed on his white T-shirt in case he did the disappearing act again. It was hard work, because the sand was loose and sliding.

"Wait up!" I panted. "Shorter legs here!"

Patrick stopped. He wasn't even breathing hard. "Am I going too fast?"

"You have, like, twenty percent more aerobic capacity than me," I said. "I did a fitness report when I was in the seventh grade." My legs were starting to feel like macaroni, so I grabbed for his hand to pull myself up the dune.

Patrick's fingers went stiff for a second, and then they curled around mine. Even against the wind, I heard him sigh.

"Still think I'm a jerk?" His voice was kind of plaintive.

I opened my mouth to say *yes*, but I found myself saying, "Umm," instead.

You gotta play it cool and keep them guessing, said Hallie's voice in my head, but what kind of loser holds hands with a jerk? I wondered what I really felt about

40

Patrick. The best answer seemed to be "insufficient data."

"Rowena?" said Patrick.

I squeezed his hand, and decided not to let it go. "I'm thinking. I'm thinking."

After that I didn't have the breath to say anything, because we were climbing an Everest made from sand. My feet kept sliding on tough, unfriendly grass.

"It's marram grass," said Patrick. "It helps to stop erosion on the dunes."

"Enough, already," I said. "*Patrick,* I'm pooped."

He looked at me sideways. "No clouds today?"

"Huh? Let's sit awhile."

We sat. The sand was cold under my butt, but my right side was warm because of Patrick. He went on holding my hand. "Do you like my beach?"

"I suppose you made it especially for me," I said, and I was only half joking.

"It isn't as simple as that."

It wouldn't be. Nothing was ever simple with Patrick Carroll.

He squeezed my hand. "Do you like it?"

I tracked three waves right into shore while I sorted my ideas. "It's neat, but kind of quiet," I said. "I thought Australian beaches were full of blond surfers."

"You've been watching too much television," said Patrick.

"You mean they're not like that?" Hallie would be gutted.

"Some are," said Patrick. "Would you rather go to a beach like that?"

41

I was starting to feel hungry, and it occurred to me it must be close to lunchtime. And at lunchtime . . . I jumped up, dragged my hand out of Patrick's, and nearly fell down the dune. "I've got to call Mom!"

"There's plenty of time. We'll be back before you know it."

"But we walked for miles and miles."

"Let's run!" Patrick got my hand again, and ran me down the dune. I could feel the rough sand under my feet, and taste the salt on my lips. We ran faster and faster, and the wind whipped tears into my eyes. It was wild, but Patrick's hand kind of anchored me. If he let go I'd fall flat on my face, and I knew it was going to hurt.

"Trust me, Ro," said Patrick. His voice came in gusts through the wind that was battering my ears. "I won't let anything hurt you while you're with me."

We hit the bottom of the dune still running, and I stumbled face-first into a big old shrub. I was untangling myself from the branches when Patrick said, "Here are your shoes." He gave me my flip-flops back, and I put them on, then followed him the few steps up the path.

Clancy Park was bright in the sunlight, and a couple of moms were pushing baby strollers along the path to the Peony Patch. Not far away, I saw a guy setting up a soft-serve stand.

"Let's go get a cone," I said. I was proud that my voice was steady as I asked the guy for a double-chocolate waffle cone. "And one for my—"

The soft serve guy raised one eyebrow. "And one for your . . . what?"

"For my . . ."

Uh-oh, raspberry Jell-O time.

"One for *him*." I nodded back toward Patrick, but Patrick wasn't there.

UNAVAILABLE.

It was no use letting a double-chocolate waffle cone melt into a puddle, so I ate it as I walked back to the house. I figured I'd earned those calories with that long hike up the dunes. I let myself in with the key, and my hand didn't shake one bit. It was right on ten after twelve, so I called Mom's cell phone. The call cut to her voice mail.

"The person you are trying to contact is unavailable. Please leave a message after the tone."

Good one, Mom. Say, *Call me,* and then be *unavailable.*

I didn't leave a message. Instead, I fixed myself some crackers. I poured some juice and took a bunch of grapes. Then I went out in the garden to have my lunch.

It was kind of like a picnic, and I wished I could share it with Patrick. I pictured him sitting with his arms around his knees, smiling in that way he had. . . .

I frowned. What way did Patrick smile? I knew he *did* smile, but did he show his teeth? Did he crinkle his eyes, or wrinkle his nose? Did he have a crooked grin

44

or was it flashy as a toothpaste commercial? Did he have a dimple?

I lowered the cracker I was about to put in my mouth.

Patrick, I thought. I could still feel the warmth of his hand, but I couldn't remember his smile.

I ran a few photo fits through my mind. Did he have an overbite? Retainers like Hallie's? Blue eyes? Brown eyes? Had he worn shades? Was he Latino?

All right, already! I told myself. I tried to center my mind.

Maybe I'd imagined it all? My mind said, *Uh-uh, no way.* I closed my eyes and remembered his hand in mine. I remembered his voice saying, *Trust me.* That was real. Patrick Carroll was real.

I wished Hallie were there to bounce things off of. *Why not?* I thought, and I sent a mind message way over the ocean to Hallie.

Ro to Mahalia Thomas. Ro to Hallie—Hallie, listen up!

I sent my mental message off to Hallie, down the Woodbrock Valley, and up the avenue to the John Stephen Apartments.

It was eight-thirty, and Hallie was messing with a makeover site on the computer. She had her tongue tip poked out, and she was guiding a pile of gold curls over a JPEG of her own cornrow braids.

"Yech, gross," I said, and Hallie's finger slipped off of the mouse.

"Hi, Ro—isn't this neat?"

"Blond is so not you. Does your mom know you're messing with her computer?"

Hallie grinned. "It's her Pilates class tonight. Met any hunks yet? Come on—dish the dirt on the boys down under."

"Nada, zilch," I said.

"Dirt or hunks?"

"Either—well, I kind of met a boy. His name is Patrick Carroll."

Hallie spun around in the chair. Her braids swung out like a carnival ride, the kind where little kids cling on seats attached to chains. The little kids squeal, and so did Hallie. "You didn't! You did? Tell me!"

"He's different . . . not just a regular boy," I said.

"How different? C'mon, dish!" Hallie was practically hissing with excitement. "Older like nineteen? Hot or not?"

I stabbed a guess. "Seventeen. Maybe." Hot didn't seem to be the word.

Hallie puffed out her cheeks and pretended to wipe off her forehead. "Whew! Older guys are trouble. Where'd he take you? What'd you do?"

"The beach," I said. It was like talking through a mouthful of cheese.

"The beach?" Hallie pounced. "How are his abs or—"

Her voice broke off, and she did the braid-swing thing again. "Major bummer!" she said. "Gotta go. Mom's at the door." The monitor went blank, and she shot across the room and hit the sofa.

Ms. Thomas came in, and looked around the room.

"Mahalia Aretha Thomas, have you been messing with my computer?"

"Like, yeah?" said Hallie.

Ms. Thomas clicked her tongue. "Mahalia Thomas, you are so dead!"

I giggled. Those two are such a double act, you wouldn't believe it.

"So sue me," said Hallie. *"How was Pilates, Mom? Got any more cool moves?"*

The John Stephen Apartments faded out, and I opened my eyes. I was still in the garden. I'd known that all along. Hanging with Hallie in a mind message wasn't the same as being with Patrick Carroll at the ocean beach, but it kind of creeped me out. I'd been using Hallie like a kind of puppet, testing her reaction to the boy down under.

"Patrick," I whispered. "Patrick Carroll." I heard my voice no louder than a breath. "Patrick," I said, a teensy bit louder. "Patrick Carroll."

I picked up the cracker and ate it, and then I drank some juice. My throat was dry after all that salty air. I wriggled my toes and imagined the grittiness of sand. "Patrick?" I said in my regular voice, just to prove I could.

I picked up my plate and juice glass, and took them into the kitchen. I did the dishes in the sink. No dishwasher. Would you believe it? While I dried them, I looked out across the garden.

Patrick Carroll was leaning on the gate.

I slung the dishtowel and marched out of the house. "What are you doing here?" I tried to sound like Mom in kick-butt Dr. Maven mode, but my voice came out like *Ro is pleased to see you.*

"I brought you this." He was holding the driftwood I'd picked up at Ocean Beach. "You dropped it when we climbed the dunes. Do you want it?"

I took it from him and rubbed it on my cheek. It felt silky and smooth and real. I wanted it, but I was suspicious. If the wizard of the Roach Hotel had planted a forty-mile beach in my mind, he could easily plant the idea of a piece of driftwood. I almost told him where to put his souvenir.

Cool it, Ro. It's not like the guy is giving you his class ring, or asking you home for Thanksgiving.

"Thanks," I said. "How did you find me?"

"You're staying here—aren't you? Renting this house?"

"But how did you *know*?"

His eyes went blank, just for a second, and then he smiled. "You told me."

"I did not," I said. "Uh-*uh*."

"Sure you did, Rowena. You had to call your mother from the house, and this is the only house for rent in this neighborhood."

"How did you know?" I asked again. "Do you know the real estate agent?"

"There aren't many houses for rent in Clancy," said Patrick. "Most of them are flats, so logically—"

"Flat what?"

"Flats. Units. Apartments." He grinned. "Does it matter how I knew?"

"It matters," I said. "How did you find out? Exactly?"

He took my left hand in his. A kind of shiver ran down my backbone as he turned up my palm and traced the lines with his fingers.

"You have a strong head line, Rowena," he said. "It says you're analytical. You can never let things be. You have to *know*."

"Say what?" I goggled at him. He was still holding my hand and tracing my palm with his fingers, but he sounded angry. The words seemed to patter through the air like hailstones, and I could have sworn a shadow passed over the sun. I shivered.

"Never had your palm read before?" he asked.

"Why would I? It's only guessing," I said, but of course I had. Way back in fifth grade, Hallie and I had giggled over our heart lines, and tried to count the creases by our pinkies, to see how many children we'd have.

"Two point four," said Patrick.

"Huh?"

"Going by statistics, you will have two point four children," said Patrick. "That's not a guess."

"You can't have point four of a baby!"

"The statistics say you can. Does knowing that help you in any way? Are you feeling enlightened?"

"I don't know what you're talking about," I said.

"You do know, but never mind that now." He gave my hand back, but he still wasn't smiling. "Did you call your mother?"

"Yes." I didn't add that Mom had been unavailable.

Patrick was still on the other side of the gate, cut off from me by a crisscross of painted boards. I stared at his white T-shirt. It was so clean, I wondered if he'd changed it after we'd left the beach. I wondered why he'd come. He wasn't smiling, and he hadn't come in or asked me out. He seemed to be thinking hard.

"What?" I said.

Patrick jumped, and I saw his eyes change focus as he stopped staring at nothing and switched his gaze to me. "I was wondering if it was worth it."

I didn't ask what he meant. The cold feeling in the pit of my stomach told me. He was wondering if hanging with Rowena Maven was worth the hassle. I bit my tongue. If he'd been a regular guy, I'd have told him to go play in traffic, but the wizard of the Roach Hotel was not a regular guy.

"Listen up," I said. "This was your idea, if you recall. You landed on *my* balcony. I didn't climb onto yours."

My voice sounded kind of tight.

How lame is this? I asked myself. *You've seen this guy, like, three times? What is it with you? He's not to die for. You don't need this!*

"I don't need this!" I said.

Patrick went on staring. For a regular-looking guy, he could stare for the Olympics. His eyes were blue, but now I noticed dark rims around the iris and dark shadows underneath. I felt the pit of my stomach give a kind of swoop and sway, like I was riding a roller coaster. Black dots crowded in and blotted out Patrick's face.

I reached out to grab the gate, and found I was holding his hands instead. They were warm and real, and when my eyes cleared I saw his face change as the cold look disappeared. He blinked and bit his bottom lip, and then gave that cute half smile.

"I'm sorry, Rowena. That was way out of line."

"Darn right it was," I said. I threw his hands back at him.

He tucked them into his pockets, and scuffed one toe into the sidewalk. "This isn't about you; it's about—"

"*Puh-lease!*" I said. "That is so lame! If you want to break up, just do it, already!"

The words echoed in my mind like a dried pea in a can. *Break up?* How could we break up when we'd been out together *twice?*

And we hadn't gone to the movies, just to a park and the beach—places that Patrick had somehow made me see. . . . That was not a date.

I felt my face making like a tomato.

"Breaking up is what I'm trying *not* to do," said Patrick softly, and for a moment his eyes looked like a frightened little boy's. "Please, Rowena, don't give up on me."

"Give me one good reason not to!" I clenched my teeth so hard my jaw hurt.

"We both need a friend."

I nodded. He was right.

"So is it OK?" he asked. "Are we OK?"

"Kind of," I said.

"Friends?"

I shrugged. "Friends. But no more evasions. If I ask you a question I want a straight answer."

Patrick tilted his head. "I'm not hiding anything that will hurt you."

"What are you hiding it for, then?" I snapped back.

"Because it would hurt *me,*" said Patrick.

That's what I thought he said, but the telephone rang just then.

"I'll be back!" I said, because I hadn't finished with him yet.

It was Mom, of course, in full Dr. Maven mode, dissing me for not calling her at noon. I dissed her back for being unavailable, and she checked and found that her cell phone had been switched to mute. By the time we'd both apologized and I'd gone back to the garden, Patrick Carroll had gone.

51

- 7 -
LIP-ZIP.

When Mom came home, we went to the park and bought cones from the soft-serve guy. I'd already had my high-cal treat for the week, but this emotional stuff was making me hungry.

"This is the life, honey," said Mom. She'd left Dr. Maven behind on a suit hanger and shoe rack at the house.

I felt the chocolate coating of the cone crunch under my teeth. It was like walking on thin ice, like being with Patrick Carroll. I wished I could have a cell phone, but it didn't seem a good idea to mention that right now.

"How did the lecture go?" I asked instead.

Mom rolled her eyes. "Just peachy, honey. They were hanging on my every word, but underneath they were thinking, 'We didn't need a Yankee to tell us *that*.' "

"You're not a Yankee," I pointed out.

"Honey," said Mom, "to the Aussies *anyone* from the States is a Yankee."

I opened my mouth to say Patrick didn't think like

52

that, then I closed it again. I had no idea how Patrick thought.

"So, honey, how was your day?" Mom licked a smear of chocolate off of her top lip, just like Hallie does.

"I went for a walk," I said. "I kind of went to the beach."

Mom raised one eyebrow. "How can you *kind of* go to the beach? Did you take a train to Bondi?"

"A different beach." I put my hand in my pocket to touch the piece of driftwood. It felt smooth and solid, and I stole a peek to make sure it was real.

"Meet anyone interesting?" Mom looked way too curious.

"I met—" My lips came together to shape the P-word, but nothing came out. I groaned. Raspberry Jell-O time again!

Patrick, you rat! I thought. *You've been messing with my mind!*

I decided to have it out with him next time he showed. Friendship was fine and dandy, but *friends* don't stick the lip-zip lip-lock on one another, not without asking first. Not this kind of lip-lock.

My stomach lurched a bit as I thought of the other kind of lip-lock . . . but Patrick Carroll was going to have to watch his step.

As Mom and I walked back from Clancy Park, I saw a boy who might have been Patrick. He had bleached-straw hair and dark chocolate eyes, and he was scuffing his sneaker into the sidewalk. Mom must have seen me staring, because she made some dumb remark about how it was just as well Hallie wasn't here, or her hunk-o-meter would go right off of the dial.

53

I made like I hadn't heard.

When we got back to the house, the telephone rang. Mom sighed. "Get that for me, honey? It's likely Sorrel checking in."

Patrick! I thought. I walked, not ran, to the telephone. I picked up the receiver (it was so old it had a cord!) and held it to my ear.

"Hi," I said, playing it very cool.

There was a second of silence, then Hallie said, "Ro?"

I felt my eyes bug. *"Hallie?"*

There was a dead half second and then an authentic Hallie squeal. "Who else? So what's going down, Ro? Met any hunks? Can you see that bridge from your apartment?"

"Whoa!" I said. "I already told you . . ." But I hadn't told her anything, except by mind message. "Guess you didn't get my message, huh?" I said.

Pause.

"You sent me an e-mail?"

"Not exactly."

"You texted Mom?"

"No." I swiveled my eyes toward Mom. She was mouthing, *Is that Hallie?* in my direction.

I nodded yes, then turned so she couldn't read my lips. "I sent you a mind message," I mumbled.

"Say what?"

"I sent you a—"

"Cool!" said Hallie. She hummed our spooky tune. "Listen up, Ro—I got Mom entering every travel contest around."

"Neat," I said. "The mind message, though?"

It was hard to talk to her, because of the delay on

the line. It was only a half second, but it made things we said overlap at the ends.

"I guess that means you met a cute guy!" said Hallie. "How about that!"

"Hmmm," I said.

I heard a little *scritch-scratch* noise.

"You've been eating popcorn again," I said.

"Say what?"

"And now you've got it caught in your retainers. . . . I can hear you scraping it off."

"Forget the retainers, Ro . . . dish me the dirt about this guy! I bet he's got abs to die for!"

"I haven't seen them yet, but he hasn't got hairy toes."

"Cute butt?" Hallie persisted.

I groaned. Sometimes Hallie is just too much.

"He's gotta be something," said Hallie. "You've gone all quiet."

"He's . . . it's different," I said. "He's different."

"Different how? C'mon, *dish!*"

"Way different," I said.

"Different like how?" demanded Hallie. "Hot or not? You haven't found another nerd, have you?"

This was weirding me out, because Hallie sounded just the way she had when I'd mind messaged her before.

"You have!" crowed Hallie. "You've been and gone and found another nerd. Has he got your face on his screen saver too?"

"He probably hasn't even got a computer."

"So what's his name?"

My lips shaped the P-word, but the lip-zip snapped in place.

"Come on, *dish!*"

I couldn't get a word out. And then I heard Hallie give a kind of gasp. "Look, Ro—gotta go. Mom's coming."

My tongue came loose in a second. "She doesn't know you've called me? Hallie, you're going to be so dead."

"She put the egg timer on me." Hallie giggled. "She left it sunny-side up, but I turned it over easy already. Listen, Ro—you go for it. You hear what I'm saying? This guy must be something mega to make you go all quiet. . . . OK, OK, Mom—all right, already! See ya, Ro, but next time it's your turn to call. Right, Mom, I'm hanging up. This is me hanging—"

There was a scuffle and another giggle, and then Ms. Thomas came on the line. "Good night, Rowena." I heard the click as she cut the call.

"Hallie?" asked Mom.

I nodded yes.

"Her mom let her call?"

"Kind of," I said. "She had the egg timer on her, but Hallie flipped it over." I frowned. Ms. Thomas had said, *Good night Rowena,* but it was only afternoon. I counted back on my fingers and discovered it was evening back in Woodbrock. "I've been talking to yesterday," I said. "That's kind of neat."

Mom flipped on the electric kettle and looked at me sideways. "So, honey, who hasn't got a computer?"

I got this doomy feeling, because I couldn't tell her. Not with the lip-zip. Then I thought of a way around it. "Just this guy Hallie was dissing," I said.

I saw Mom shake her head. "That girl is boy-mad."

"Oh, come on, Mom, Hallie's just kind of—"

"Not that there's anything abnormal about that," said Mom hastily. "Is he cute? The guy without the computer?"

"Mom," I said, "I really can't say."

Then I thought of something else. "How would Hallie have gotten this number?"

"You didn't write her?"

I shook my head. "Did *you* send it to her, Mom?"

"No," said Mom.

"Then how did she know where to call?"

"Let's think about it. How would she?" said Mom. No, make that Dr. Marina Maven, making like an educator.

I didn't want to play this game with Mom. It was fun when I was little, but now it was a pain in the butt. "I'll ask next time," I said. "I need a cell phone."

And Mom said, "Hm. We'll see."

The next day I went to work with Mom. Dr. Maven doesn't take no for an answer. "It's a boys' school," said Mom. "A private college. That's why it's in session already. You'll find plenty of eye candy."

As if!

Mom and I caught the train on the North Shore line and rode it for seven stops. Then we got out on a quiet platform. There were pink bougainvilleas along the fence, and I could see the heat haze shimmering over the landscape. It didn't look real. I followed Mom's heels up the steps (which all wore real estate advertisements on the risers) and through the station, clop-clopping in my new pink wedges. The attendant never looked at our tickets, and Mom had to clear her throat twice before he'd take notice.

"Northcote College," said Mom.

"Give it a tick; then just follow the herd, love."

This is not the thing to say to Dr. Marina Maven, and Mom's eyes went sharp. She started tapping her toe, and I expected any minute to see steam coming out her nostrils. I was surprised the ticket guy didn't turn into a puddle of mush.

Another train pulled in, and a river of boys came pouring up the steps. They wore white shirts with a red logo, gray shorts, and straw hats.

"They don't look like college kids to me," I said.

"Northcote is a K-through-twelve college," said Mom, and we set off after the boys. I felt kind of invisible, because none of them had given me a second look. Most of them hadn't given me a first look. There was a dull roar of talk.

"Eye candy," I said to Mom. "Yeah, right. In *those* hats?"

"They have a uniform code," said Mom. "Get used to it, Ro."

"I don't have to wear that!" I guess I sounded horrified. I was thinking of the skinny jeans and cute tank top I'd worn on my first day of high school back in Woodbrock. Hallie had gone glam in satin-edged cargos and a cute blazer.

Mom laughed. "Well, no. You wear navy pants or a skirt and a light blue shirt at Clancy High. We'd better go get it when we finish here." She hiked up her briefcase, and we followed those boys about five hundred yards up the street to the school.

Northcote College was 120 years old. The buildings were brick, and there were boys all over; all of them were dressed the same. I checked faces over in case

Patrick was there. Then I wondered if I'd recognize him anyway.

A blast of music sent boys toward the entrances. In less than three minutes they'd all gone, except for one little blond-haired kid who looked like he might start crying anytime.

Mom stopped a yard away from him, like teachers always do. "Hello."

He stared at her. His hat was too big, slipping off of his head.

"It would be neat if you could take us to the office."

The kid nodded. We were halfway across the quad when a teacher came out. "There you are, Jarred! Tim was looking out for you." She glanced at Mom and me. "I'm Bridie Kitson, the junior coordinator. You must be Dr. Craig and . . . ?"

"Dr. Craig couldn't make it," said Mom. She did not look pleased. "I'm Marina Maven. I guess you weren't told about the change?"

"Oh!" Ms. Kitson looked embarrassed. "I do beg your pardon, Ms. . . ."

"Dr. Maven," said Mom. "This is my daughter, Rowena." She gave the Dr. Maven kick-butt smile. "I take it you're familiar with the John Smith case?"

"Run along to Ms. Borojavic's room, Jarred," said Ms. Kitson to the kid.

"Thank you, Jarred," said Mom.

Ms. Kitson glanced at me, then turned to Mom. "Sorry about the mix-up, Dr Maven. I'll find those case notes. If you can shed any light . . ."

Mom jerked her head to me, but I stayed where I was. "I'll come find you later."

I watched them disappear into the college. No way did I want to get ignored by those boys.

I walked the paths a while. I imagined hundreds of boys doing math and world studies behind the walls. Finally I sat on a seat under a big old oak. I wished Mom hadn't mentioned school. I closed my eyes and tried to pretend I'd be back at little old Woodbrock Senior High. Wouldn't Hallie just freak if I showed on Monday, like I'd never been away? That wasn't going to happen. I'd be turning up at Clancy High next week.

It had seemed a cool idea, but what if C.H. was like *this* school? What if the kids all blew me off?

I got goose bumps. I should have found out who was hot or not. . . .

Don't make friends with any Desperate Debbies, said Hallie's voice in my mind. Great advice, but how do you know the Desperate Debbies from the Popular Princesses when you first walk into a school?

My eyes blurred in a kind of panic, and I shivered and rubbed at my arms. An acorn bounced on the ground in front of me.

"Goose walk over your grave, Rowena?"

Patrick Carroll was perched in the tree, holding another acorn ready to drop.

"Why am I not surprised to find you here?" I said.

"Why would you be?" said Patrick. "Catch, Rowena!" He dropped a leaf this time. It spiraled down on the little old breeze, and I caught it out of the air.

"That's one happy day," he said. "Look after it. They don't come very often."

"Say what?"

Patrick smiled. "It's an old tradition. Catching a leaf before it touches the ground gives you a happy day. Coming up?"

"You come down."

"Stand clear. It wouldn't give you a happy day if you tried to catch me."

He dropped out of the tree and landed neatly in front of me, and I looked him up and down. Same blue jeans, same white tee, same running shoes. "Don't you ever wear anything else?" I asked.

Patrick looked down at himself. "What would you like me to wear?"

I tried to imagine him in a school uniform, but the picture wouldn't come. I tried to dress him in pants and combat shirts like Josh and Tav wore at home in Woodbrock. And I tried to put him in a Woodbrock tee and baseball cap like Tedson Wallace wore. None of it fit. I absolutely couldn't imagine Patrick Carroll in any other clothes.

"Whatever," I said. "I just wondered."

"I don't have to think about these," said Patrick.

I stared at the white tee. Climbing the oak and jumping down hadn't left a mark on it. Nor had walking miles of Ocean Beach. It was weird, but this was Patrick Carroll. Weird went with the territory.

"What do you wear to school?" I asked.

"This."

"Say what?"

"This is a school. I'm wearing this. Are you pleased to see me?"

"What do you wear to your school?"

"Are you pleased to see me?"

"Yes," I said. "If you must know. I've been so bored I'd be pleased to see Count Drac—"

Patrick laid his fingers against my mouth. "Don't say that! Be careful what you wish for."

I folded my arms. "You're a genie, right? You can grant my wish? Puh-*lease.*"

"I'm no genie."

"Only a hypnotist, right?" I said. "What's with the lip-zip you slapped on me?"

Patrick tried that cute grin again. "Sorry about that, Rowena."

I kicked at his shin, but my wedge went flying off my foot. "That's no answer."

"It's all you're going to get."

I glared at him, but my mouth kept trying to turn up at the corners.

"Smile," he said. "You know you want to."

"You are impossible," I said. I scuffed my wedge back onto my foot.

"I've often suspected that," said Patrick. "Where shall we go today?"

"I can't go anywhere. I've got to wait for Mom."

"You'd be back in plenty of time," said Patrick, "but it's your call, Ro. See you."

"Uh-*uh,*" I said. "What's wrong with hanging here?"

"I know somewhere cool," said Patrick.

"You would." I gave up, because Patrick was right. I could always tell him to go away, but why should I? The down under boys weren't lining up to know Rowena Maven. Neither were the down under girls. "OK! Let's go somewhere cool, but don't forget I've got to be back to meet Mom. Otherwise I'm toast."

- 8 -

UNMISSED KISSES.

Patrick took me down the path that ought to have led to the station. Instead we came to a river that wound and splashed between trees and boulders. The trees were hung with long strands of moss like the hanks of raffia Beth Anne's mom used for weaving.

"Where are we meant to be this time?" I asked. It was green and gloomy under the trees, but I felt cool spray coming off of the water.

"Meander," said Patrick. "Downstream from the falls." He sat on a gray boulder and took off his shoes to dangle his feet in the water. "Still think my feet are hot?"

"As if." I dipped my hand in the stream. I could feel the current tugging at my fingers. A chill ran up my arm and the goose bumps came again. "No one could have hot feet here," I said. "This water is freezing."

"We could go somewhere warm if you want to swim."

"In these?" I pointed at my capri pants and tank top. "It wouldn't be a good look if I showed up at that college dripping wet."

"Tell your mother you went swimming."

"With the wizard of the Roach Hotel. Take the lip-zip off of me and I will."

"You could swim in your underwear," said Patrick.

I stared at him. He stared back with innocent puppy-dog eyes.

"Or I could find you some bathers. . . ."

"No way, José." I was not putting on a swimsuit flimflammed up by Patrick. It might turn out to be the emperor's new clothes.

"Bring your swimming things next time. *And* proper shoes." He pulled his feet out of the water. His toes hadn't even gone blue. "Let's see what's upstream."

The trees were gnarled and lumpy with age. Some had lumps on the lumps, and others had dropped branches across the boulders. It was hard hiking in my wedges, and I soon got green smears on my capris.

"Wait up," said Patrick. He bent and grabbed my ankle. "Give me your foot, Ro."

"Why . . ." I hopped and grabbed his shoulders to catch my balance.

"Give me your foot! Unless you've got more blood than you need."

"Blood?" I twisted to look at my ankle, and out of the corner of my eye I saw Patrick flick away something small and black. "Yech! What was that?"

"Just a leech. The snake in paradise. Don't you know your old stories?"

"A *leech?* Yech! You've got *leeches* here?" I felt sick to my stomach. I hate leeches like I hate roaches.

"It hadn't got attached." He let go of my foot. "I told you to watch what you said."

"Say what?"

"Back at the school," he reminded. "You were saying you'd be pleased to see—"

"You mean Count Drac—"

Patrick muzzled me again with one hand. "I told you not to say that!"

I pried his hand away from my face, and kept hold of it in case he tried again. "That's got nothing to do with *leeches*— Hey—whoa, Nellie!"

"Right," said Patrick. "They both suck blood. But the leech didn't get any, so you won't turn into one."

"Why should I turn into— Oh, you're yanking my chain."

He grinned. "Just a bit. But you're quite OK. OK?"

I swallowed three times. "I guess."

Patrick held my hand and I let my feet do the walking while I kept a watch out for bloodsuckers great and small.

We were hiking down a little trail when a drop of water plopped into my eye. I wiped and checked, in case a seagull had plopped on me.

"It's rain," said Patrick. "You'll get wet after all."

Another drop splashed on the top of my head, cold through my hair, and a third one hit my cheek. With a hiss the rain spattered down through the trees and made dimples and rings on the surface of the river.

"Great!" I said, as my bangs commenced to drip. "Not. You mean you can't control the weather?"

"It's better when I don't," said Patrick. "We can find shelter." He tugged at my hand, and we started off at a slithering run.

Mental note, Ro, I thought. *Don't wear wedges when you go out with Patrick Carroll! He's into some serious hiking.*

65

"Trainers are better for most places," said Patrick.

The rain was sheeting down now, but Patrick jumped off the trail, crouched, and pulled me after him into a shelter. When I shook the water out of my eyes we were hunkered against a huge fallen tree. The trunk had hit a humongous boulder, and made a kind of cave. Patrick was laughing, and I saw drops of water clinging to his eyelashes before he wiped his face on his arm.

"This wasn't part of the script," he said. "What now, Ro? Play 'I Spy'?"

"I guess we wait for it to stop," I said.

Patrick shook a spatter of rain off his hair. "You wishing you'd stayed at that school? Or told me to get lost?"

"I'm thinking. I'm thinking."

He looked really hurt. "If you have to think about it . . ."

"I've thought," I said. "I'd have to be dumb to prefer squooshing up here with you to broiling back there by myself." I pulled at the tank top, which was sticking to me. Most boys would have been staring at my chest, but Patrick was watching my face. I took a deep breath. "Guess I'm dumb, huh?"

"Guess we both are," said Patrick. He kind of gathered me in and kissed my nose, then leaned back to look at me. "Say something, Ro."

"You missed," I said. It wasn't the smartest retort, but it was all I could think of.

"I never miss," said Patrick.

"You did so miss. But it could have been worse. At least we didn't get our retainers locked together," I said. "That's what happened to Hallie when she played 'Spin the Bottle' with Tedson Wallace at Halloween. Beth Anne and I thought they were having this big old kiss and all the time they were gridlocked. It took three dental hygienists with drills to get them undone."

Patrick grinned. "That's a lie. And who's Hallie?"

"My best buddy back home. Would I lie to you?"

"Yes." He leaned in closer.

"OK, so it took one dental hygienist, with a kind of little pick. But she was one mean mama." I was babbling on, because I wasn't ready to have him kiss me again, in case he didn't miss. I kept on hearing Hallie's voice in my head: *Older guys are trouble.*

"Ro—"

I ducked my head, and my cheek came up against Patrick's shirt. I could feel his heart beating underneath, and I wanted to wrap my arms around him. But this wasn't "Spin the Bottle," with the whole of ninth grade cheering and clapping. This was some faraway place that didn't exist. That's when I noticed something else.

"What?" asked Patrick as I pulled back. "No chance of a gridlock here. Neither of us has a mouthful of metal."

"Your shirt is dry."

"Is it?" He sounded puzzled, like I was changing the subject.

I looked hard, but there was none of that kind of translucent look white shirts get when they're wet.

Patrick pinched some of the fabric, pulled it out, and let it snap back into place. "So it's dry. How is that bad?"

"We were out in the rain."

He shrugged. "It's drip-dry. It dripped. It dried. Or else I ran between the drops. I'm really, really agile. What is it with you and this T-shirt, Rowena? You seem to have an obsession with appearance."

I stared at him.

He cocked his head. "It's only a shirt, like a hundred other shirts. Cheap as chips, probably made in China. Does it matter if it's wet or dry?"

"Guess not."

"You don't sound sure." The smile was gone from his eyes.

"I guess it doesn't matter," I said. "You're weird, Patrick Carroll, but that doesn't matter either." I wanted to bring the smile back, so I added, "I still say you missed."

Patrick leaned in, then suddenly changed direction and kissed my ear. My head rang like someone had clanged cymbals. "Patrick, you—"

"Jerk," he said. "I didn't miss that time, either." He peeked past me. "Rain's stopped, Ro. We'd better go back." He got up and pulled me after him out of the cave.

Outside, there was a clean smell in the air, raindrops were all over the moss, and mist was rising from the water.

"That's clouds being born," said Patrick. "Shall we walk on them?"

I thought about walking on mist or clouds, and my stomach kind of jolted. I didn't know if I was more scared he could do it, or that he couldn't. "Not today."

"I wouldn't let you fall," said Patrick. "Mind out!"

"Yech!" I ducked and shut my eyes as a fringe of

long moss flopped onto my face. By the time I clawed it away, we were back at Northcote College.

"Wear bathers next time," said Patrick, and turned away.

I grabbed at his arm. "Say what? When's next time?"

"You'll know," said Patrick. "Close your eyes."

"Why?"

"Trust me."

When a guy says that . . . I closed my eyes. Patrick brushed my cheek with his fingers, then kissed my nose again. "Didn't miss that time, either," I heard him say, but when I opened my eyes he'd gone.

Mom was in the auditorium, talking to a boy with red hair. It looked kind of serious, but Mom snapped out of it when she saw me.

"Just in time, Rowena," she said. "You want to pick up a snack at the cafeteria? Tim will show you. Tim, would you show Rowena—"

"Sure," said the boy.

I thought about picking up a snack while all those boys pretended I didn't exist. "I guess I'll pass," I said.

"Sure, honey?"

It should have weirded me out to hear Mom's Mom-mode voice coming from Dr. Maven, but I was beyond that now.

"So," said Mom, "did you find something to do?"

"There was a boy in one of the trees," I said.

I was surprised when that came out. I'd expected the lip-zip to snap into place.

"One of the little tackers, I guess. He'll cop it from Kitson," said the boy. "Rena, you—"

69

"Was he wearing the Northcote uniform?" put in Mom. "You get a lot of nonconformity here?" she asked the boy.

"Only old Petey." The boy looked confused, but I was used to Dr. Maven and her three-way conversations.

"He was wearing—" Raspberry Jell-O time again. And I couldn't remember what Patrick had been wearing. I just knew it wasn't a Northcote uniform, because I couldn't picture Patrick in any kind of uniform.

I couldn't picture Patrick at all.

"He wasn't a college boy," I said to Mom, "and anyway, he's gone."

But he'll be back, I promised myself. *Somewhere. Sometime.*

Mom turned back to the redheaded boy to grill him some more, and I walked back to the station.

I sat on a white-painted seat and kicked my heels. I watched the heat shimmer above the lines, and thought about Patrick Carroll. Not the way he looked, of course, but the way he *was.* Lame jokes, kind of sensitive, sweet and . . .

My mind felt like pulled taffy as I tried to think why he might want to hang with Rowena Maven.

I wondered where he'd show up next.

You'll know, said Patrick's voice in my head, and I smiled in the sun. Our dates weren't the kind kids had back in Woodbrock, but how was that bad? So I missed out on minigolf, movies, and burgers at Greedy Gus? Instead, I climbed dunes and saw clouds being born. And got kissed in a tree trunk cave.

"*I'VE GOT A HOLD ON YOU.*"

Clancy High looked like a regular school, but kind of empty, because classes weren't in session yet. When I'd gotten my uniform and courses, we met Ms. Eckhart, who was going to be my homeroom teacher.

I wanted to ask where the cool kids hung out, but I didn't want Mom dissing me later, so I asked about elective courses instead. Mom mentioned progressive student-directed learning, and I tuned out and thought about mossy boulders and Patrick Carroll.

"Think you'll like it, honey?" asked Mom as we walked back to the house.

How could I tell? School is all about the people, not the place. "I guess I'll be way behind in some courses," I said.

"And maybe way ahead in others. You've done three months of high school already, if you recall. If you don't understand something, ask."

"They'll think I'm dumb."

"You'll be dumb if you don't. What you get out of this experience is up to you."

On Friday afternoon, I met Patrick at the milk bar. (That's what they call a corner store down under.) I'd gone for a fizzy drink (that's what they call a soda), and Patrick was waiting when I came out. His face lit up when he saw me, and I guess mine did the same.

"I've got my swimsuit," I said. I wore it every time I left the house.

Patrick took my hand. "Where to, Ro?"

"The best place to swim." I pretended I was giving orders to a limousine driver.

"Yes, ma'am!" said Patrick, and we started walking.

"I've got an hour, is all," I said.

"No problem," said Patrick. "We'll just go earlier."

It was hot, and the sidewalk felt sticky under my flip-flops. And then the sidewalk turned black, like tar, and we were walking through tropical trees. The sun jumped, and the heat came down like a blanket. Perspiration prickled out on my lip.

"Where's the pool?" I said.

"Just up this path." Patrick squeezed my hand. "This is the *best* place, Ro."

I plodded beside him. "It's up a mountain?"

"It's called Rockslides. Don't worry. There aren't any crocs."

"Crocs?" I said. "Like, crocodiles?" Even I knew there aren't any crocodiles in Sydney, except at the zoo.

"Like, crocodiles," agreed Patrick. "See those signs? If there were crocs, they'd carry warnings."

The signs did carry warnings—about the rocks. They repeated the warning in German. GEFHAR. DANGER.

Like, you could end up dead?

"Here we are," said Patrick.

I stepped off the trail and onto a long, gray slope of

rock, with trees growing right out of it. There were hills on either side, and the high valley echoed with the dashing, splashing sound of water as a mass of little waterfalls and cascades fell over the smooth rocks and into a series of pools.

I picked my way down the slope to the first pool. It was about ten feet across and thirty long, with a baby waterfall at one end and a narrow channel leading out of the other. It was soooo beautiful.

Patrick was taking his shoes off, so I kicked off my flip-flops and shucked my pants and tank, and splashed right on into the water in my bikini.

It was colder than I expected, and I yelped.

I heard Patrick laugh behind me. "You'll warm up, Ro. Just give it a chance."

I rolled over and kicked some water at him. "You taking that shirt off, or what?"

Patrick looked down at himself. "I guess so," he said. "Maybe."

"I won't peek," I said. "This is me, not peeking." I rolled over on my stomach, and balanced my hands on the smooth bottom, letting my legs float in the water. The current tugged at me, and Patrick was right: It wasn't so cold anymore. "How deep does it get?" I asked.

Patrick didn't answer, so I forgot about not peeking and shuffled around to sit in the water. "Patrick?"

"Over here, Ro!"

Patrick was sitting on a rock in the waterfall, with the white water smashing and splashing over his shoulders and trying to force him off of the rock.

He was still wearing that darned white shirt. It was

wet now, anyway, molding around him so it looked like part of the water.

"How did you get there?" I yelled. "You were just behind me."

"Come on," Patrick yelled back, "it's great!" He reached both hands out to me and the force of the water drove him into the pool, just like a slippery slide. He sank and then came up, bubbling. "Come on, Ro!" He reached for me again.

I shook my head. I wasn't sure I was up for that.

Patrick stood up, pouring water. "Grab my hand, and we'll get to the rock I was on before."

"The rock you were washed off of before," I reminded.

"Come on, mermaid," said Patrick. He was laughing. I grabbed his hands and let him tow me in toward the rock. The current was fighting against us, trying to pull us apart, but together we struggled right up to the falls. They were only six feet high, but there was plenty of water coming down.

"Up you go," said Patrick. He grabbed my hips and boosted me up on the rock, then swung up beside me. He put an arm around me and grabbed hold of the rock on the other side. We were wedged into place like we were sitting in a cable car, and the falls were beating against our backs like a Jacuzzi turned up to the max.

"See?" said Patrick right up against my ear. "If we stay close, you and I are a match for anything."

"Great," I yelled back, "but how do we get off?"

Patrick took his arm away. Next thing, he whooshed away down the current and disappeared in the whirling foam.

I tried to stay put, but the water pushed me clean off the rocks. Patrick caught me around the waist before I could sink.

"Hold on," he said in my ear. He pushed off into the current, and we went swooshing through the pool, shot down the channel, and splashed into the second pool.

"Wow!" I said, when I could get my breath. My legs and arms felt as if I'd swum a mile. This pool was much deeper, and away from the channel the water was almost still.

"Float a bit," said Patrick.

"I can't. My legs sink. So does my head, and I get water up my nose."

"You must be going about it the wrong way. Just roll over as if you were lying in bed. I won't let you sink."

"You won't be able to stop me," I said.

"Trust me," said Patrick. He swam behind me. "Come on, Ro. Just lie back."

"I'm sinking." I kicked my feet up.

"Lie still." I could feel Patrick's fingers gently on my temples, and his thumbs were behind my head. "Now, take a long, slow breath. Not too deep."

I did as he said, and I actually felt my body rise in the water.

"Let it out, just as slow, and you'll sink just a bit," said Patrick. "Now, in, out, in, out . . . see how you can control it? Close your eyes and just let your body float. . . ." I felt his fingers drawing gently away from my head, and I was about to yell at him for letting go when I realized he hadn't been holding me up anyway.

"That's right," said Patrick. "You're doing it by yourself. Roll over now."

I felt a bit dizzy from all that deep breathing, so Patrick steered me to the edge, then boosted me up to sit on the hot stone shelf.

I thought he'd join me, but he dived to the bottom like a dolphin. The water was so clear I could see him ten feet down, twisting and darting among the rocks. He looked like some kind of merman, if mermen wear blue jeans and a white T-shirt.

I leaned back on the smooth rock and felt the slanting sun on my face. The sky was a deep, strong blue, like sapphires or the delphiniums Aunt Vida grows against her stucco wall. There were a few pale pink clouds, and it seemed quite early in the day.

And that was when I remembered we weren't really there.

"Patrick?" I said.

He was cruising the pool like a seal, and he had something in his hand.

"You haven't caught a fish?" I leaned over to see.

Patrick leaned his elbows on the ledge. "This is for you," he said, and dropped a pebble in my hand. It was a little round stone, dark flinty gray with paler streaks, like the rocks I was sitting on. I kept hold of it even after we'd walked back to the milk bar in Clancy.

"Patrick?" I said.

"Ro?" He was dry and regular looking, and his white T-shirt looked as if it had been laundered and tumbled dry, or bought brand-new from the store. I brushed my fingers over the sleeve, and it wasn't even one bit damp.

"I have to start school next Tuesday," I said.

He nodded.

"I won't be seeing you in class, will I?"

"No, Rowena." His eyes flickered away over my shoulder as if he were looking to escape. I tugged on his sleeve to focus his attention.

"I'm not asking where you go to school, but how can I get ahold of you?"

"You can't."

"I can!" I tugged on the shirt again. "I've got ahold of you now, Patrick Carroll."

"Have you?"

My hand closed on empty air. "Well, I did," I said.

"Maybe I've got ahold of you," said Patrick, and I felt his hands on my waist. Then he bent and kissed the side of my mouth.

"Darn it," he said, "I missed." And then he wasn't there.

Back at the house, Mom looked at me hard. "You caught the sun, honey."

"I guess," I said.

"Have you met anyone from your new school yet?"

I shook my head no.

"You'll find your feet," said Mom. "I know you've been lonesome so far, but things will change when you get to school."

I went into the bathroom and looked at my reflection in the mirror. I tried to imagine Patrick standing behind me, bending to kiss me the way he had just now.

"Patrick," I said. I half closed my eyes, but I couldn't see him, even in memory. He'd slipped away again. "But I've got a hold on you," I said.

I felt in my pants pocket for the stone from the bottom of the Rockslides pool.

That weekend Mom and I went to Bondi Beach. There were lots of little kids rushing around with water wings on their arms, and older kids hanging out or kind of eyeing one another. Three girls who looked like bikini models came parading by as though the sand were a catwalk, and spread themselves out on towels. There were boys playing beach volleyball, and the ball always seemed to land right near the bikini queens. The bikini queens pretended not to see.

"Go say hello, honey," said Mom. "Seems like they might be in your classes."

"Mom, there are one hundred eighty high schools in Sydney," I said. "Why should those girls be at Clancy High? This is Bondi."

Mom pushed her shades up her nose. "I guess you're right, honey, but don't fret. Ms. Eckhart thinks you'll fit right in."

"Where did you get that from?" I asked.

"They had exchange students from Dallas, Texas, last year, and a boy from Guatemala."

I rolled my eyes. I've never been to Texas, or to Guatemala.

"Say hi, anyway," said Mom. She gave me a little push. "Go on, honey. You've been here three weeks and hardly spoken to one person under thirty." She smiled. "Except the tree boy at Northcote. Was he cute?"

It wasn't only the lip-zip that made me frown at Mom. She might be an educational behaviorist, but she knows *nada* about the modern dating scene. She thinks she does. She asks my opinions, but she mostly doesn't care for what I say.

"Listen up, Mom," I said. "Back home you call Hallie boy-mad when she says a boy has a cute butt, and now you're asking me if a boy I talked to up a tree for, like, two minutes, was cute. How is that consistent? And do you see any other person my age here with her *mom*?"

Mom got up and brushed sand off of herself. "Someone's been eating grumpy fruit," she said. "I'm going back to the house. You can catch a train later. I'd hate to cramp your style."

I wondered why I was so hog-stubborn. I knew I should say hi to those girls, or even just smile. At worst they'd blow me off; at best I could pick up on the local scene.

So do it, already!

I turned to look at them, but they had their heads together over a magazine, filling out little check boxes.

"It'd be neat if Hallie were here," I said.

Mom looked down at me. "How would it be neat?"

"We could hang out like that," I said. I nodded toward the bikini queens.

"And you'd have said hi to those girls if Hallie *had* been here, right?"

I pictured Hallie sitting cross-legged beside me in her candy-pink swimsuit, flashing her million-dollar mouthful at the boys. Give her five minutes and she'd have them eating out of her hand. But hang with the bikini queens? Not Hallie.

"I thought not," said Mom. Her voice was so dry it was, like, straight from Death Valley. "So it's as well Hallie isn't here."

I stared at Mom.

"Think about it, honey," said Mom. "Aren't you two just a bit overexclusive? Maybe it's time you stepped out from her shadow and learned to function without her."

Mom walked off, leaving me in shock. I could not *believe* Mom. First she dissed Hallie for being "boy-mad" and now she said the two of us were "over-exclusive"? Where did that come from? Hallie and I are best buddies, but we've got other friends. Like . . . well, like Beth Anne, Josh and Alex, Shonee, Tav, and Tedson Wallace the Third. We've known one another forever.

I started wondering which was my best friend, after Hallie. Beth Anne thinks magazine quizzes are a waste of time. Josh is kind of dumb, and Alex is a nerd. I remembered Hallie saying Alex had a crush on me.

Yech.

Shonee is the ninth-grade beauty queen. Not a zit in sight, a chest that all the boys stare at. She's been dating since seventh grade. Hallie says Tav must be short on brain cells. He never says squat in class, but he's a jock, so it doesn't matter. And as for Tedson Wallace, after the retainer gridlock he never looks right at Hallie anymore, and that means he blows me off as well.

Who else was there—Doughy Chloe? Puh-*lease*.

Maybe Mom was right. Maybe Hallie wasn't just my best, but my only friend.

I dug my fingers in the sand. It felt gritty and rough, not like the fine white sand at Ocean Beach.

Patrick. I got a rush of goose bumps down my arms. If I told Mom I had a boyfriend, she'd have to accept that I was doing fine away from Hallie. But there was the lip-zip thing, and even if I could tell Mom, she'd be antsy about my dating a stranger.

I sifted some sand through my fingers. Next time Patrick said, *Where to, Ro?* I'd say, *I want you to meet my mom.* Then Mom would get off of my case.

I was thinking how to convince Patrick when someone kicked a spray of sand up into my face.

"Sorry. Oh, hi, Rena!"

I smiled up, because I thought it was Patrick, and found myself eyeballing this strange boy. He had red hair sticking up in tufts, and invisible eyelashes. He was wearing sagging blue swimming trunks and he had a white strip of zinc cream over his nose. I didn't think he was Patrick, but who else knew my name?

"Do I know you?" I asked.

Good one, Ro. How lame is that? But what if you kiss the wrong guy?

The boy frowned. "You are Rena, aren't you? Dr. Maben's kid? I saw you sitting with her just now."

I stared at him.

"You came to our school, Northcote College? Dr. Maben asked me to take you to the canteen and to show you round, only you nicked off while she was talking to me."

"Oh," I said. "My name's Rowena. That was you talking to Mom?"

"Yeah, about Petey. He used to go to Northcote—"

"Before he went psycho," said one of the other boys.

Tim took a swing at him. "Shut up."

I saw one of the bikini queens whispering something to the others, and they all cracked up.

81

"Give it up, retard. The chick doesn't want to know you," said one.

"Rack off, Claire," said the boy. What was his name—Tim? He gave me an injured look. "Sorry I spoke."

I waited to see if the bikini queens would say something to me, but they went back to their magazine. Then I thought I'd say something to Tim, but he'd gone off along the beach.

I went back to trickling sand. Good old Ro. Total social fiasco. Tim seemed OK, but I didn't want to be with a guy with spiky red hair. I wanted to be with Patrick.

- 10 -

SCHOOL DAZE.

On my first day at Clancy High, Mom handed me a little packet.

"What's this? A brown-bag lunch?"

"Open it," said Mom.

It was a cell phone—but not the cool kind.

"It's prepaid," said Mom. "You have fifteen dollars of credit for the week. That's plenty to send me a text if you're running late, but not enough to call Hallie every five minutes."

"As if!"

"I'm not saying you can't call her," said Mom. "Just giving you the facts. After this week, I'll give you that amount of credit every two weeks, and if you need more you can pay for it out of your allowance."

"Neat, Mom." I could see her waiting for me to show enthusiasm, so I started scrolling through the options and testing ring tones.

"Don't play games when you're in class," said Mom. "And keep it switched off until lunchtime. And don't leave it lying about."

"Anything else?" It was neat to be connected to the

83

world. It would have been neater if Mom had let me pick the style of handset I wanted.

Mom smiled. "I'm sure you'll use it responsibly. And call me at lunchtime, OK? If you sign up for any after-school activities, let me know what time you'll be home."

"I'll text you," I said. "Thanks, Mom."

Mom relaxed and gave me a hug. "I'll see you after school, honey."

Clancy High wasn't far from Clancy Park. I peeked over the fence as I passed, kind of hoping Patrick would be there to wish me luck. I hadn't seen him since our swim. I missed him, and I knew it would totally raise my image if my boyfriend walked me to school on my first day.

I pictured us walking up to the gate, then Patrick kissing me good-bye and going off . . . where? I could not imagine Patrick going to a regular school.

But now I could text him and arrange a date.

Dream on, Ro.

I walked as slowly as I could, but Patrick didn't show.

The school grounds were filled with kids of all ages, from seventh graders to seniors, like it was junior and senior high mixed up on one campus. I thought of taking out my cell, making like I was chatting to a guy as I walked. Then I thought, *How lame is that?*

I found the office, and asked for Ms. Eckhart's room.

The secretary, Ms. Chong, looked at me over her glasses like I was a bear escaped from the zoo.

"Rowena Maven?" She sorted through admissions. "You're the transfer student from the U.S.," she said, like it was news to me.

I nodded.

"One of the girls will take you to your homeroom." Ms. Chong rapped on the glass window of her office and beckoned. "Claire Tilley! Over here."

Claire Tilley was taller than me, and had a piercing in her eyebrow. Her hair had tips and streaks, and she managed to make the uniform look glam. "Yes, Ms. Chong?"

"Claire, Ms. Eckhart has you for homeroom, doesn't she?"

"Yeah."

"Then take Rowena with you. She's just starting today."

The girl kind of glanced at me and sighed. "Yes, Ms. Chong." Then she jerked her head. "Come on, Ena."

"Rowena," I said. "Or Ro."

She started pushing along the hallway so fast I could hardly keep up. "You in year nine? Got a locker yet?"

"I was in ninth grade back home," I said.

Claire turned and stared at me. "You American or something?"

I nodded yes.

"Haven't I seen you around?"

My spirits sank down into my shoes, because Claire Tilley was one of the bikini queens I'd seen on Saturday. She knew me, too. I saw it dawning in her eyes.

"I get it. You're the chick Dim Tim was sussing out down at Bondi! You want to watch him; he's a gunna."

"Say what?"

"Gunna do this, gunna do that." She laughed like she'd said something witty. "They're all losers at that snob school, anyway. Half of 'em are spaz-brains. Can't get by in a *real* school. You know one of Dim Tim's mates hasn't been in school for a *year*? He just sits in his apartment—if Cam or I pulled something like that we'd get the kid cops round."

"How do you know him if he's such a dumb-ass?" I asked, to turn the tables.

"He's my cousin, the wanker. So, um, what's your name again?"

"Rowena Maven," I said.

"What are you doing in this hole? Did— Wait up, Leah. *Leah!* Wait up! Look here, Rowena, I'll catch you later, OK? Just go on up this corridor and in at Room KE-nine. Ask Ecky to sort you out with a locker. Leah! Wait up!"

Claire scooted off, and I stared after her. That girl could talk up a storm. I wondered if she'd blown me off on purpose. I knew what Hallie would have called her—"Airheaded Claire."

I found my way to Room KE9. Ms. Eckhart was sitting at a table, not taking one scrap of notice of the riot in the room. I kind of hovered at the door until an older girl came over. She had zits and that studious look the brains always have.

"Are you looking for us?"

"I guess," I said. "Ms. Chong said I was to come to Room KE-nine."

Ms. Eckhart beckoned me closer. "Nice to see you made it, Rowena. Find yourself a desk—anywhere will do. Have you got a locker yet?"

"No, I—"

"We'll see to it later," said Ms. Eckhart. "Just sit

down for now, because the music will start any tick of the clock—"

Right then the music did start, blaring out of a speaker. I didn't recognize the band, but one girl said, "That's *so* last year."

The music died, and most people sat down. Ms. Eckhart looked us over and gave a kind of grim nod. "I see the usual suspects sitting with other usual suspects. As usual."

Someone giggled, but most of the guys groaned.

"You can sit where you please for the first week," said Ms. Eckhart, "but next week will see some changes . . . Ah, Claire! How kind of you to join us."

Claire had come in, and was grinning at another girl across the room. "Ta, Ms. Eckhart. I had to see Leah about something important. I'll sit . . ." She let her voice trail off, and looked about. I saw some girls shuffle up to make room for her.

Okaaay, I thought. *Claire is no Desperate Debbie; she's a Popular Princess.* Then I saw the zit girl roll her eyes.

"All right!" said Ms. Eckhart. "Now that the late Ms. Tilley has joined us, we can get under way. Most of you know the way I operate in homeroom, but for the benefit of the year sevens and other newcomers, I'll run through things again.

"Homeroom is the place you come first each day, and the gathering point when you come back from your last class of the day. As your homeroom teacher, I am responsible for passing on information and answering any questions. Any *sensible* questions, Cameron."

"Awww . . ." said one of the boys.

"If you have any problems with work, or with anyone at this school, I am your first port of call. I'll help if I can, or refer you to the appropriate person. Sometimes that will be a peer counselor, a tutor, or another teacher. There is also a guidance counselor for more difficult matters. That's all I'm going to say about that for now, except for this: In Clancy High no one is left to struggle on alone. We have an excellent student support network and we want you to use it."

"Or else," said the boy who had groaned before.

"Or else," agreed Ms. Eckhart. "Before we go on to sorting out timetables and homework diaries, I'd like to introduce Rowena Maven. Rowena has come to us from Woodbrock in the United States and will be spending some months at Clancy. I know you will all welcome her and do your best to make her stay a pleasant one."

I cringed in my seat.

Clancy High had about six hundred kids, and it took me a while to get a hold on things. The courses had different names. The ninth graders didn't know squat about the War Between the States, but I felt dumb when someone mentioned the Tasmanian devil. I thought that was a myth.

I had gotten acquainted with some people, but I hadn't made any proper friends. A few in my year stood out as popular or desperate. Airhead Claire was OK, but flaky. One day she'd be acting like we were best buddies; the next she'd blow me off while she went rushing off after Leah or Cam or Tai or one of the other cool people.

Cam was the year-nine wise guy. If you laughed at his jokes he was OK with you, but if you teased him he'd say something cutting. He was always mimicking me, and if I thought I sounded like that, I'd take a vow of silence. The zitty, brainy girl, Luisa, turned out to be Claire's older sister, and wasn't desperate. She had a dry way of talking that I kind of liked, but she was a year twelve, so I only got to see her at homeroom, or in the library. She had a study buddy called Maria, and they were mostly together.

I guess that was the problem. Most people at Clancy High had a social life already. To get a place in the pack I'd have to shuffle someone out of the way, and I didn't want to look like a Desperate Debbie. No one dissed me, but I felt like I was on a high wire. One false step would have me fall on my butt.

I wished I could text Hallie at lunchtimes, but she didn't have a cell phone. On Friday, I decided to call instead. It was ten after twelve, and I sneaked into the shed where the janitor keeps the grass trimmers. I closed the door and sat on a big ball of twine. It took a couple of tries to get the international number, and then it was ringing, back in yesterday.

"Thomas apartment, Mahalia sp—"

"Hallie, hi!"

There was this little pause, then the authentic Hallie squeal. "Ro! Buddy! What's new? Where you calling from?" Her voice washed over me like a long, cold soda, and I felt myself relax. I hadn't known until then how the Aussie accent had been grating on my nerves.

"I'm at school," I said to Hallie. "Tucked away in the janitor's shed."

Hallie giggled. "With your hunk, I hope?"

"I should be so lucky. Listen up, Hallie, how did you get our house number?"

"That'd be telling."

"Come on, give!" I said.

"I asked Mom for the name of your mom's agent. And then I called him and asked for your number in Australia."

"You got it from *Wilf*?" I could not believe it. Wilf never gives anything away.

"Like taking candy from a baby. So, Ro, what's new? You're calling from the janitor's shed—hey, that means you got a *cell*?"

"Enough, already!" I said. "There's not much going down, Hallie. I'm kind of trying to catch up on things at school. I did get a cell, only I can't talk for long. And—"

"Tell me about your hunk. Where do you hang out?"

"We went swimming at a place called Rockslides," I said. "It was the *best*. P—" *Snap!* The lip-zip slotted into place.

"Send me some pix. You met other cool people?" Hallie filled the silence. "I'm jealous like you wouldn't believe. You'd better not like them more than you like me. . . ."

"As if!" I said. "So, how's Beth Anne . . ." I paused, and waited for Hallie to chime in.

"Josh and Alex and Shonee, Tav and Tedson Wallace the Third," we chanted together.

"Same old, same old," said Hallie. "Little old Tedson still blows me off and—"

"Hello, Ro."

"Say what?" I spun around, still hearing Hallie

rattling away in my ear. There, leaning on the janitor's door, was Patrick Carroll.

"If you're busy, I can go," said Patrick.

"No, you wait right where you are—"

"I'm not going anywhere," said Hallie.

"Not you; I'm talking to . . . to—"

The lip-zip was still in place, and I reached out to grab Patrick by the sleeve. "Get this thing off of me!"

"I can't," said Patrick.

"But—"

"Earth to Ro, Earth to Ro . . ." said Hallie. "Who's that with you? I do not believe a sexy janitor . . . what'll your hunk say?"

"No," I said. "It's . . . Someone has come in, is all. My . . . I mean, a boy—"

"Sounds like you could use some privacy, but mind, I want to know *all*," said Hallie. "Listen up, Ro, I can call you in a few days, Mom says. If you haven't got a hot date, I'll call at . . . Sunday before noon?"

"That's Monday here," I said. "Count fifteen hours . . . Hallie . . . *Hallie?*" I was talking to empty air.

"Sorry about that, Ro," said Patrick.

I wasn't sorry. I couldn't help a big grin spreading across my face. "Hey, Patrick, guess what?"

Patrick folded his arms across that darned white shirt, and grinned back. "What?"

I waved my cell. "I can text you, or even call. Is that neat or what?" I got off of the twine ball and held out my cell. "Want to be the first number on my list?"

Patrick didn't take the phone. "You know I can't do that," he said.

I clamped my mouth shut. Pleading with a boy is not a good look.

91

"It's not that I don't want to be with you, Ro."

"So it's OK for you to come see me when *you* want," I said, "but *I* have to wait on your convenience."

"You can always tell me to go," he said. "You're under no obligation to see me."

I was about to say I hadn't meant that, when I caught on to what was happening. "You always throw me that line, Patrick Carroll, but it's not gonna work anytime soon. Are you some control freak?"

Patrick was looking someplace between me and him. I don't know what he saw, but it didn't seem to please him.

I grabbed his arm to focus his attention. I could feel the tendons all hard and stretched, and though I was ticked off with him, I wanted to rub them smooth.

"All right, Rowena." His voice seemed to come from someplace cold. "I do make some rules. It has to be like that. If I lose control . . ."

"What?" I shook his arm.

"I don't dare," said Patrick.

He slid down the wall, and wound up sitting with his legs straight out, like a rag doll. I sat with him.

"You're creeping me out," I said. "You're not on some medication, are you?" I looked at him hard. I knew he wasn't what Hallie would call a hunk, but his face was part of my landscape.

He shook his head. "I *want* to be with you, Ro, but if you need a boyfriend you can SMS, or wear on your arm, or discuss with your friends, you'll have to find him somewhere else."

"That's giving it to me straight," I said. "Your rules or nothing. What kind of relationship is that?" My chest felt funny and I couldn't get my breath.

Patrick gave me the shadow of his cute smile. "It's the only kind I can have."

"*Why* do you want to see me? If it's so hard on you?"

"You ground me," said Patrick.

"Huh?"

"You're my anchor." He put his arm around me, and I leaned against him. I wasn't sure about the anchor bit, but the hug was warm and real. "Ro, you know any myths?"

"Guess not," I said, although I could kind of recall a few from my elementary school days. "What's SMS mean?"

Patrick gave me a better smile. "Small Message Service. You might text your friends on a cell. *We* SMS our friends on a mobile."

"Only you *don't*," I pointed out.

"Well, no. Where shall we go?"

"I have to be back in class in a half hour."

"You've got time. Trust me."

"I guess," I said, although it wasn't a question.

Patrick got up and held out his hands to me. I let him hike me up; then I brushed some old grass clippings off of my pants, and followed Patrick out of the janitor's shed.

Cam and Claire were messing about outside, sharing an MP3 player, one earpiece each. Cam was singing along, and Claire was slapping at him like he was a pesky mosquito.

Claire saw me right away. "You don't want to let old Jackman catch you in there," she said. "He doesn't want anyone getting into his pot plant . . . ation."

"Okaaay," I said. I waited for her to fix on Patrick, but she didn't glance at him.

"What were you doing in there?" asked Cam.

"Talking." Out of the corner of my eye, I saw Patrick moving on. He looked like he was no one in particular going nowhere much. "Hey, wait up!" I called.

"Talking to the Weedwacker?" Claire giggled. "You're one weird chick, Rowena."

"Cute, but . . .," said Cam, and Claire made a grab at *his* butt.

"Whatever," I said. I ran to catch up with Patrick, and next thing I was crunching along on some hard, rough ground in broiling sun, and Clancy High was nowhere.

- 11 -
OUTSIDE ALICE.

"Where are we?" I asked. The scenery did not look promising.

"We're somewhere outside Alice," said Patrick.

"You got another girl out here?" I didn't like that notion one bit. Patrick Carroll was one weird guy, but he was *my* weird guy.

"Alice Springs," said Patrick. "It's a city in the outback."

I kind of translated what he said in my mind. "Like, the outback is desert? Someplace like Salt Lake City in Utah?"

"Alice is the nearest city to Uluru."

I couldn't see any city. There were hills in the distance, and a few stunted trees, and everything looked kind of red-colored, like the terra-cotta pots Beth Anne's mom sells at Woodbrock Mart.

" 'Near' can mean a week's hike in the outback," said Patrick. "Do you like it, Ro?"

"It's kind of empty."

"Not when you know how to look. See that thorny devil?"

I couldn't see a thing but red dirt and rock, but Patrick pointed with a twig and I made out a little reptile sunning itself on a rock. It was blotched with shades of brown, and it had spines all over. It looked like some cute little dragon.

"That's so neat!" I was going for a closer peek when I kicked something white. It kind of rolled. "Yech!" I said. "What died?"

"Kangaroo, probably." Patrick came and stood by me. "Everything dies sometime, and out here nothing gets wasted. See?" He pointed with the twig. "See those ants? They've polished that skull up nice and clean. Pretty soon the old thorny devil will eat some of *them,* and so it goes on."

"Yech," I said again.

"You've never eaten kangaroo? Or croc burger?"

"No way, José! You gotta be joking!"

Patrick shrugged. "It's no different from eating venison. Or lobster."

"Crocodile?"

"You never had a croc burger with lettuce and mayo?"

"OK, wise guy," I said. "Have *you?*"

Patrick started to nod, still grinning; then a kind of shadow came over his eyes.

I prodded him in the ribs. "Was that a yes or a no?"

"I don't . . . I think . . ." Patrick's voice kind of faded and he wasn't there anymore.

I sighed. This disappearing trick was too much. I wanted to call out for him, but I thought I wouldn't give him the satisfaction. I picked up a round stone half the size of my fist and tossed it at the skull. The thorny devil never moved from its perch.

I quit standing around after a while, and sat on a rock. Then I hugged my knees and put my head down to keep the sun off of my face. I could feel the perspiration making my school shirt stick to my back, and I was kind of thirsty.

I'll count back from ten, I decided. *Then when I get to zero, Patrick will be back.*

I started to count, but I never got past four. I guess I was scared of what would happen if he didn't come.

You're way out here in the desert, I thought. *You could die of thirst and turn into ant food, just like that kangaroo. Some individual might find your skull all polished by the ants.*

Then I remembered I wasn't really there. This was someplace Patrick had invented.

So look and see where you really *are,* I told myself.

I set my elbows on my knees and stared out across the red desert.

It's not empty if you know how to look, said Patrick's voice in my mind, so I squinched my eyes and tried to see what he meant. There was a heat haze shimmer over the ground. There was a twisted tree that hardly cast a pinch of shade. There were the hills, red like a painting. . . . And I saw a neat little twister come dancing and twirling across the plain. It sashayed left and right, and picked up dust and twigs in its center.

I stared hard enough to make my eyes tear, and then I caught sight of Patrick, way off in the distance. He was standing with his hands in his pockets, and he looked so lonesome I stopped being mad at him.

While I waited for him, I took out my cell phone and keyed in Hallie's number.

It wouldn't connect.

"Isn't that just peachy," I said aloud; then I tucked away the cell phone and went back to the good old mind-message routine.

Ro to Mahalia Thomas . . . Ro to Hallie, come in! Say something, Hallie, please.

I pictured the message zapping Hallie right between the eyes—*ker-pow!*—and I saw her run her fingers over her cornrows the way she has when she's wondering if maybe it's time they were redone. It takes hours to braid them all, and I sit with her sometimes while it happens.

Beth Anne can sit with you this time, I said.

Uh-uh, not her, said Hallie. *She's, like, "Why don't you get it done in regular braids and save yourself three hours and fourteen minutes?"*

So why don't you?

Hallie made bug eyes at me and shook her head. *Uh-uh. So, Ro, what's with the sexy janitor? Don't you forget I told you older guys are trouble.*

There's no janitor; it was Patrick again.

A giggle from Hallie, and she commenced to sing: *Rowena and Patrick up in a tree, kiss, kiss, kiss, kiss kissing!*

All right, already! I said. *We were talking. Just talking.*

Why? asked Hallie.

We talk a lot. We argue.

Blow him off, said Hallie. *You don't need that.*

I can't blow him off. I love him. . . .

That thought came so suddenly that it jerked me right out of my mind-message mode.

"I didn't see that coming," I said aloud.

"Didn't see what, Ro?" Patrick was back beside me.

"You want to see the Todd River? That's really something!"

"What is it with you and water?" I couldn't look at him, in case he read my face.

"I like it," he said. "Water turns into clouds, and then back to rain. And then—"

"Do I look like I want a meteor lesson?" I folded my hands and primmed up my mouth. "This is me, wanting a meteor lesson."

Patrick stared at me. "What did you say?"

"This is me, wanting a meteor lesson—"

"That's what I thought you said." He put his arm around me. "Why not? Hold tight! Now *bring it on!*"

The sky went black, as if a big storm were coming. The shadow raced over the desert and I saw the thorny devil disappear. "What—" I said, but Patrick gave me a squeeze.

"Watch the skies, Ro. See—there's one!"

I watched the skies like he said, and out of the clouds I saw this orange-yellow light. It skimmed across the black, and a bluish-green trail streaked after it. It had hardly died away when another one followed.

"What are they?" I asked. "It isn't the Fourth of July, but is someone letting off fireworks?"

"It's the Leonids," said Patrick in my ear. "A meteor shower."

"Meteors?" I yelped. "Don't they, like, make massive craters in the ground? And flatten bits of Siberia?"

"Not the Leonids. Keep on watching!"

I watched until my eyes were burning, and I found I was shivering with cold. It was so quiet I could hear blood pumping in my veins, and the steady beat of Patrick's heart. I imagined I could hear the hiss of the Leonid shower like a splatter of rain coming in through forest, but the sound was all in my mind.

I was soon stiff-legged from standing, and Patrick must have felt the same, because he sat and pulled me down into his lap.

"What do you think of it?" he asked in a low voice, like he didn't want to break the desert silence.

"They're neat," I said. I wanted to say more, but I couldn't think how to say it. I knew Patrick was showing me something special, but I hoped we weren't in Siberia. "What's with the cold?" I asked. I rubbed at the goose bumps on my arms.

"It's always cold in the desert at night," said Patrick. "You want to go back now?"

"I guess." I nodded against his shoulder. I could have sat there forever, but time was passing, and I had to—

"I'm supposed to be in math!" I said. "I'm toast!"

"Oops . . ." said Patrick. He was laughing. "Will I be toast too, for keeping you out all night?"

"Say what?"

He kissed my left eyebrow. "Don't worry, Ro. You haven't missed a class. We'll just back up the time a bit. Come on!" He stood up and spilled me out of his lap. My feet were cold and stiff like wooden blocks, but we walked a few steps and then we were back near the janitor's shed. There were plenty of kids hanging around, but none of them looked at Patrick and me.

"Groundsman," said Patrick. He grinned at me. "We call him a groundsman, or a caretaker, not a janitor."

"Whatever," I said. "Did I ask you?" I could feel the

cold rising off of my skin like a mist, and a shiver ran down my spine.

"Goose walk over your grave, Rowena?"

"Just answer me one thing, Patrick," I said quietly, so no one would overhear.

Patrick looked wary. His eyes skittered off over my shoulder the way they had when he didn't want to hear what I was going to say.

I prodded him. "Why the sky show? I thought we were going to see a river? The Todd, you said."

"You said you wanted a meteor lesson." He held out his hands. "I reckon you meant a meteorological lesson, but who am I to argue the toss?"

"You're jerking my chain."

"Just a bit. You'd better go into class."

"When you've gone," I said.

"That's now. Consider me"—Patrick leaned in and dropped one of his kisses on my nose—"gone," said his voice from the air, because he had disappeared.

The music blared out from the speakers. I looked at my watch and calculated I'd been with Patrick for half an hour, three hours, or maybe half a night. I couldn't be sure, but it hadn't been long enough for me.

In science that afternoon, Mr. Diver started to talk about time and relativity, and I thought, *Hey, this is all about Patrick!* I doodled our initials on my scratch paper: *PC4RM.* It was kind of liberating to see that school hours wouldn't keep me from going out with Patrick.

- 12 -

GETTING FRESH ON THE MOUNTAIN.

Some days, it seemed that Mom and I had always lived in the house in Clancy, and that I'd always gone to Clancy High.

Other days, I'd wake up expecting to see the posters on the wall in our Woodbrock apartment, and to hear old Mr. Abrahams calling his cat in the brownstone across the road.

Back in little old Woodbrock, it was winter, coming into spring.

Here in Clancy, it was summer, heading into fall.

Back in Woodbrock, there were Hallie, Beth Anne, Josh and Alex, Shonee, Tav, and Tedson Wallace the Third. Oh, and Doughy Chloe.

Here in Clancy, there were flaky Claire, Leah and Renae, Cam, Tai and Luisa, Maria, and all the others from the school.

And here there was Patrick Carroll. My boy down under, the wizard of the Roach Hotel.

I could never say when I'd be meeting Patrick, where it would be, or where we'd go, but it was always someplace I didn't expect. One thing kept me from daydreaming overmuch: It's kind of a chore to focus your mind when you can't recall a face.

Whenever I began to see a pattern, it would skitter sideways out of reach. I wanted to pin Patrick down like a butterfly on a board, but butterflies on boards will never fly again.

I tried to tell him that once when we were watching a geyser spurting way high in the air.

"But why, Ro?" he asked.

I licked my lips, tasting the faint salt of the spray. "How would *you* like it if you didn't understand who I was and where I was coming from, and if I wouldn't tell you?"

"I don't need to know," said Patrick. "You're Ro. My girl. You're my anchor, and my link. . . ."

"To what?" I asked when he didn't finish the sentence. I nudged him with my elbow, in case he was about to fade out again.

Patrick put his arms around me. "I won't hurt you. You know that, right?"

"Sure, I know that," I said. "But—" *But couples share things,* I wanted to say, but I couldn't say Patrick didn't share things with me. He shared geysers and deserts, wildflowers, endless beaches, and showers of meteors. He shared swimming holes and weird rock formations. Once we spent half a night in a cave where the Aboriginal Australians used to camp out in bad weather. Maybe they weren't the kinds of things Cameron shared with Claire, but I knew they were kind of special.

Over the weekend, Mom rented a coupe and drove us into the Blue Mountains.

"It's so peaceful to get out of the city," Mom said. We were standing on a scenic lookout. "We must do this more often, honey. It's easy to put things off."

"This is only our second month down under, Mom," I reminded her.

"That's right, honey, but time will fly, and then before we know it, we'll be on the airplane home without seeing half the things we planned."

"We won't see much if you work all the time," I said.

Mom frowned slightly. "The education system is a bit different here, but the problems are the same."

"What problems?"

Mom flapped her hand in the air as if she were swatting a bug. "Oh, you know, honey. Some gap is identified, we plug it, and a new gap forms somewhere else. Funds get channeled into one area, and another gets a little threadbare. Every dime on IndiTarg means one dime less for regular classes."

"Kind of like a dam," I said. "You plug one leak, and another starts up."

"That's the trouble with papering over cracks," said Patrick, and leaned on the fence beside me. I glanced at Mom, but she was making room for some Japanese tourists. The guides were wearing white shirts with a logo, and Patrick kind of blended in.

"You've got some audacity," I said, though my heart was dancing hip-hop because he was there. "You gonna say hi to Mom?"

Patrick looked straight at Mom. "If she says it first." He sneaked an arm around my waist.

"Don't get fresh," I said, as he kissed the side of my neck. It felt kind of weird to stand next to Patrick in such a public place. I tried to compose something to say when Mom saw me being smooched by this boy she'd never heard of.

Hey, Mom, I rehearsed. *This is Patrick Carroll. He's the oak-tree guy from Northcote College. . . . He's some kind of wizard, and he's snapped this bizarre lip-zip on me to stop me from talking about him.*

Like Mom would swallow that? She'd have me in therapy until I was ninety.

"Patrick," I said. I was warning him off, but he tickled my neck with a piece of grass. "You are so dead," I muttered.

"I'm not at all *dead,*" said Patrick. "You're keeping me alive!"

I swung my hip against him, to make him back off. He let go of me, and then Mom turned around. I waited for her to tell me to quit acting fresh, but she just smiled past me. "Are we in your way?"

I thought she was talking to Patrick, but when I looked, I saw three young guys beside me. They had dark pants and white shirts. One had a baseball cap, and a tat on his arm. One was kind of blond, with a ponytail and a nose ring, and the other had short brown hair. And which was Patrick?

I stared at all three, and felt a butterfly of annoyance in my chest. Seeing Patrick and not knowing him was worse than not seeing him. Then the boy with brown hair smiled straight at me, and winked. My heartbeat quieted down, and I tucked my hand into his arm.

"Told you I was a chameleon, Ro," said Patrick in my ear. "Now you see me, now you—"

"No, you don't!" I said. I'd gotten a good grip on his

105

arm. "What are you doing here, anyway? Are you with these tourists?"

"You were thinking of me, so I came," he said.

"You wish!"

"What were you thinking of, then, Ro?"

I sent my mind back a way. "Dams," I said. "I was thinking how you can stop water in one hole and it will sneak through another way."

"There," said Patrick, squeezing my hand in his arm, "you *were* thinking of me."

"You're weird, Patrick Carroll," I said out of the corner of my mouth. "What do you think of that?"

Mom turned again. "What was that, honey?"

I shrugged, watching Patrick move away. He gave me a sassy salute, then kind of blended into the tour group. They were all getting back in their coach, and when it pulled away, Patrick had gone.

As Mom drove us down from the mountains, I tested her for Patrick awareness. "Mom, you recall those guys with the Japanese tour?"

Mom nodded yes, never taking her gaze off of the winding road.

"How many of them were there?" I asked.

"Who knows, honey? I wasn't especially taking note."

"Did you see the one who was standing next to me?"

"The cute one with the long blond hair?" Mom peeked sideways at me. "And where would *he* have rated on Hallie Thomas's hunk-o-meter?"

I was disappointed, somehow. I'd lost my mind's eye view of Patrick, but I was pretty certain he didn't have long blond hair.

* * *

I didn't buy Patrick a Valentine; I *baked* him one instead. I bought a heart-shaped cookie cutter and made a batch of cookies. Mom might have had something to say about me baking up a storm for a boy, but she'd gone to a seminar in Melbourne.

"Am I coming too?" I asked.

"Not this time," said Mom . . . no, make that Dr. Maven. "You've just gotten settled at school. Sorrel will sleep over, or you can stay over with Ms. Tilley's girls."

"Who?"

"Luisa and Claire."

I stared at Mom. She thought I wanted to sleep over at Airhead Claire's? Ms. Tilley was one of the guidance counselors at Clancy High, but I hadn't known she was Luisa and Claire's mom. Anyway, the idea of living with Airhead Claire for a week was kind of tiring. She is *such* a motormouth.

"I'll be fine here," I said without too much hope.

"Staying alone is not an option," said Mom. "I've got something planned for just the two of us at Easter vacation, but for now, choose one of the options I gave you."

I thought about Patrick. If he'd been a regular kind of boyfriend, I'd have invited him over for a quiet dinner while Mom was away. With the wizard of the Roach Hotel, it didn't matter whether Mom was away or not. He could have walked me right out of math between one problem and the next, and no one would ever notice. They would have thought I'd gone to the bathroom, is all.

"Guess Sorrel can sleep over," I said. "Or I could go to her place after dinner."

"She'd better come here," said Mom.

* * *

I didn't look forward to having a sitter, but Sorrel didn't trouble me. She came over after dinner and watched TV or studied until bedtime. She slept in Mom's room, then left right after breakfast.

"You can always reach me on my mobile other times," she said when she left on Monday, "but I expect you'll enjoy the freedom?"

"You bet!" I said.

Sorrel laughed. "Spoken like a true Aussie."

She came back when I was baking the Valentine cookies. "Yum! Are you making them for anyone special, Rowena?"

I expected the lip-zip to snap into place, but it didn't. Could be because I didn't try to use the P-word. "I'm giving some to a guy, instead of a Valentine card," I said.

"Great idea," said Sorrel. "Most blokes would rather feast their guts than their eyes. Is he nice to you?"

That question kind of surprised me. Most people would have said, "Is he hot?" or, "Is he cute?" or even, "Where does he go to school?"

"I guess . . . I guess he tries to be," I said.

It was after I'd packed five cookies into a heart-shaped box that I wondered if Patrick liked cookies.

- 13 -

WAKE-UP CALL IN SAINT VALENTINE'S GARDEN.

It was a humid night, and I was in that sticky gray place where you can't sleep. I kept seeing the digits change on my clock. Sometimes I'd see every minute dissolve into the next; other times I'd wake and fifteen minutes had passed.

I lay still, but that made me feel like a mummy going moldy in a tomb.

"Yech!" I said aloud. I got out and fixed myself a glass of juice. Then I parted the curtains and looked out into the moonlight.

It's Valentine's Day, I thought, and I stared at the full-blown moon. It hung in the sky like a golden dollar. I couldn't see any stars. . . .

Grandpa Maven always used to send valentines when I was a kid, but I was too old now. I could see me sitting in homeroom later on today, and maybe being the only girl who didn't get a valentine.

Patrick?

I could not imagine the wizard of the Roach Hotel with a store-bought valentine or a box of candy, but he *might* send flowers. Or maybe a thorny devil.

I opened the window. The security mesh was in place, but some fresh air crept in.

"Ro?"

It was Patrick's voice, but I couldn't see him.

"Where are you?" I called softly. A warm feeling washed over me. It had nothing to do with the humid air.

Out by the garden gate a firefly of light flickered into being.

Patrick had lit a candle as a guide? I caught myself smiling. It was just the kind of fool thing he'd do. I put on my bathrobe and picked up the box of cookies.

I thought he might go before I could get outside, but when I unbolted the door, the candle still winked. I was about to run to the gate when caution stirred. What was I doing out alone in the night in a strange city? Patrick would never hurt me (so I thought then), but what if it was someone else, pretending to be Patrick? A stalker? A mugger?

I stood on the step, staring at the candle so hard my eyes began to tear.

What are you doing, *Ro?* I thought. *Are you crazy? Do you want to become a statistic?*

"Patrick?" I called.

"Here, Ro. Just outside your gate."

That *was* Patrick's voice. I was certain.

"Come where I can see you," I said.

"Into your garden?"

"Of course, into the garden, you loon!" I said. "Where did you think I meant?"

I heard the faint *skreek* of the gate as he came on through. He came closer, stopped two yards away, then set the candle on the path. He turned around slowly, with his hands held away from his sides. "Satisfied I'm me?" he asked.

I nodded yes. "I couldn't see you. You could have been anyone," I said. I pushed the cookie box into the crossover of my robe, and held out my arms. "Happy Valentine's Day!" I reached up to kiss him, and heard the box scrunch a bit.

"What's that?" asked Patrick, prodding with his first finger. "Are you wearing armor under that dressing gown?"

"I baked you some cookies." I felt myself blushing.

I was about to start walking with him when I thought of something new. Mom would not be pleased if she knew I was going off in the night with a guy. Especially in my bathrobe and baby-doll pajamas.

"Patrick—"

"We're going into daylight," he said. "It's not a good place in the dark."

"Well . . ."

"Trust me, Ro."

"I do," I said. "But I want to get changed."

"You look fine to me," said Patrick. "Cute."

"I want to get changed."

I thought he might get impatient, but he just shrugged and sat on the doorstep. "See you soon."

"You'll wait?"

"Ro, I just said I would."

I crept back through the house and changed into my capri pants and a tee. I put my hair in bunches, then took it out again. I fiddled with my bangs, and then got worried in case Patrick had gotten tired of waiting. I picked up the cookie box, smoothed it out as best I could, then went out again.

Patrick was where I had left him. He didn't look at his watch like most guys do. Not that he was wearing one. He seemed to have gotten rid of the candle. He got up and tugged at my hand. "Come on!"

"All right, already!" I fell into step beside him, and we walked down the path and out the gate, crossed the street, and turned left into a rose garden.

I felt my mouth drop open, and I guess my eyes were as wide as my mouth. "Patrick, it's . . . it's . . ." I couldn't think of anything to say.

"Do you like it?" asked Patrick.

"Oh, yes!" That was true, but I just couldn't believe this. Most places Patrick took me seemed absolutely real, but this rose garden could never have been true. It was a *Sleeping Beauty* garden, *a Secret Garden* garden, enclosed by a high stone wall that looked like it had soaked up the sun and rain for a hundred years. There were rosebushes all over, but not like anyone had laid them out in rows. Some were bushy thickets, where you could hide a horse, and others were climbing up the wall, splashing it with color like spilled paint. There were knee-high rosebushes, with teeny leaves as shiny as emeralds, and some that were kind of shaped like umbrellas, and some flowers with five petals and some that might have had sixty-five or more. They were all colors, too—red and white, yellow and pink, peach and purple and striped, plain and ruffled like the skirts of Mom's old prom dress. They didn't look real, but the smell was a natural rose smell . . . not the kind you get in perfume bottles. The only sound I could hear was a kind of busy buzzing.

"Bees!" I jumped back as a humongous bee the size of a quarter went zooming past my ear.

"Don't panic, Ro," said Patrick. "They're much more interested in the roses than they are in you. Come and sit down."

I let him lead me through the roses, ducking under wandering sprays of leaves and flowers. Once I had to stop while Patrick unhooked my hair from a bunch of thorns. I could see why he said it was no place to visit at night. We stopped at a weird little fountain, with a bowl of cherries and grapes next to the mossy base.

I put the box of cookies beside the bowl. I thought they'd probably be crumbled and broken round the edges, and I wished I hadn't made them.

"Don't!" I said as Patrick sat down and reached for the lid. "You don't have to eat them if they're all mashed up. I figured—"

"Much more practical than shiny pink cards," said Patrick. "Not that I got any cards. Did you?" He took a cookie out of the box and turned it around. "It looks like a map of Tasmania," he said, and put it in his mouth.

"They're Valentine cookies," I said. "We used to bake them in elementary school." I grabbed up a bunch of grapes, to give myself something to do, and started picking them off, one by one.

Patrick laughed. "We made pizzas, and the topping fell through the dough because we didn't have time to cook them for long enough. You'd never know cheese could drip so far down a school bag. . . ."

"You made pizza in elementary school?"

Patrick must have caught me staring at him, because

he raised one eyebrow. "What? You look as if you've seen a ghost."

"It's only that that's the first thing you ever told me about yourself," I said.

"I've been telling you about me ever since we met. Are you going to eat those grapes, or just admire them?"

I crammed some into my mouth, then handed a bunch to Patrick. I wanted to feed them to him, but what if he thought that was lame? I ate some cherries instead. "Where did you get these things? I don't see any stores."

"Off the trees and vines around the back of this garden," said Patrick, propping himself on one elbow. "There are some apples, too, if you like." He reached up and hung two pairs of cherries over my ears.

I pulled them free, and went to put them in my mouth. Then I hesitated . . . but I'd eaten some, so it was too late already. Patrick laughed, and reached across to tickle my cheek with his fingertip.

"Don't worry, Ro. You're not Persephone, my name isn't Pluto, and this isn't Hades. Do you really believe I'd play a nasty trick like that? I think I'm insulted."

I found myself smiling at how stupid I'd been. Patrick was wearing his usual blue jeans and white tee, and I'd never seen anyone less like a frowning Greek god. *No,* I thought, *you wouldn't have to use tricks to get a girl.*

Then I wondered. . . .

"Patrick, where is this place?" I asked.

"It's Saint Valentine's Garden," said Patrick. He reached up and picked a pink rose from the bush above us. "You're my valentine, Ro."

I took the rose. It had thorns, but they were up at the other end of the stem. I looked into its gold heart, half-hidden among the curling petals.

"Why this rose?" I asked. I hoped Patrick would say something romantic, like how the rose reminded him of me. I really needed him to say something romantic, something I could recall when I was old.

Dream on, Ro.

What he actually said was, "It's the one that I could reach."

Then he pulled me down and gave me a kiss . . . a proper one, tasting of cherry juice. It started off light and playful, like Patrick's kisses always were, and then it got kind of serious.

I'd read about kisses that make you feel weak at the knees, but I'd never really believed in them. Anyway, I was lying down. Would I have gone weak at the knees if I'd been standing? I don't know, but whatever it was sure sent me a wake-up call.

Patrick must have felt me start to shake, because he stopped, and rubbed his finger over my lips.

"We could stay here all day if you like. See those clouds? We could walk up there."

It took me two tries to get an answer out, and when I did it was a stammer. "M-maybe it's time I left."

"Maybe you're right," said Patrick.

So we did.

What would have happened if we'd stayed? I guess things might have gotten even more complicated than they did already.

I put the rose in a glass of water by my bed, then went to the washroom and stared at the mirror. The same old Ro looked back. Plain brown hair, brown

115

eyes, a pink tee, and olive capris. My face was a bit flushed from the Australian sun, and I didn't look like anyone's valentine. I didn't look like a girl who could walk on clouds. I looked like a scruffy kid.

Older guys are trouble, said Hallie's voice in my mind, but I pushed it away.

I smelled the scent of my rose as soon as I woke. It was going to be a scorcher of a day. Sorrel was drinking coffee in the kitchen. I fixed myself a cup and ate a piece of toast.

Claire had a KISS ME button on her shirt when I got to school, but Ms. Eckhart made her take it off. Some of the other girls had candy or cards on their tables.

"Nothing from your boyfriend, Ro?" asked Tai. "I thought you Americans made a big thing out of Valentine's Day?"

I grinned at her. "How's this scenario?" I said. "We went on a date to this lush garden of roses, and he fed me cherries and grapes, and then gave me a great big kiss and a rose."

There was a little silence; then Claire giggled.

"You're cracking me up, Ro," said Tai. "What did you give *him?*"

Wait for it, I thought. *Wait . . . for . . . it. . . .* I grinned and said, "A cookie," and that got another laugh.

It felt good to be part of the in group, but later, during math, I started to feel as if I'd kind of betrayed Patrick. The picnic in the rose garden hadn't *been* like that. I wished I'd held my tongue.

At lunchtime I went to the library so I wouldn't have

to face Tai and the others. They'd be asking for details, trying to trip me up in my own story. They hadn't really believed it.

Luisa and Maria were there, hanging over one computer, but Mr. Beck, the librarian, said I could use the other one. In the first week of the semester, he'd had us all set up e-mail accounts using the school ISP. We could use them when we had free time.

I sat down and opened my e-mail account, and typed in Hallie's addy, Hallie@gracethomas.com

I stared at the blank screen some, without really seeing it, and then started to type: *Hallie, you'll never guess where Osytovl . . .*

My fingers kind of stuttered as I saw what I'd keyed in. *Osytovl?* What was that?

I deleted it and tried again.

. . . Osytovl took me for my Valentine surprise . . .

I looked back along the line, and there it was again. *Osytovl.*

It looked like some weird Russian name.

I was about to delete and try a third time when I realized what had happened. I'd been trying to type *Patrick,* and the lip-zip had snapped into place. Only it wasn't the lip-zip, but a kind of key lock or finger lock. That darned computer would not let me key in Patrick's name.

"Okaaay," I said. I keyed in *my boyfriend* instead, and that turned out the way it should.

Hi, Hallie, you'll never guess where my boyfriend took me for my Valentine surprise. He knows this

really neat garden, full of roses and with the cutest fountain. It was really romantic. He even gave me a pink rose, and kissed me.

Remember those cookies we used to bake when we were in elementary school? I baked some for Osytovl, and he said he'd never had anything like them. Guess not. And before you say one thing, let me tell you they turned out just fine. I even put silver sprinkles on them, and not to hide the burned bits.

How was your Valentine's Day?

Mail me when you get this. I can read it on the library 'puter.

Ro ☺

I was going to read over the e-mail before I sent it, but the music started, so I pressed send, then scooted off for English Studies.

BONDI.

Hallie e-mailed two days later.

Rowena.maven@Clancyhigh.gov.au
Neat! You're on e-mail . . . zat a school addy?
>you'll never guess where my boyfriend took me
>for my Valentine surprise. He knows this really
>neat garden, full of roses and with the cutest
>fountain. It was really romantic. He even gave
>me a pink rose, and kissed me.
I told you, you gotta watch those older guys. You
give them a kiss and next they're playing tonsil
hockey or groping your chest.
So come on. What was it like? Dish!
>I baked some for Osytovl, and he said he'd never
>had anything like them.
What the heck kind of name is OSYTOVL? And
how come you were off in a rose garden, any-
ways? Where was your mom while this was going
on? Did you cut class? Seems this guy is always
taking you off alone. Don't you guys ever go to

the movies or eat at Greedy Gus like a regular couple?
>How was your Valentine's Day?
Just peachy. I got a candy heart from that squirt in that advanced math class.
Send me some pix when you can. I wanna see this hunk.
Hallie.

I was about to e-mail Hallie back and say we didn't *always* go off alone, when I realized we did. Sure, we met outside the milk bar and in the Blue Mountains, but when we went out we always went on our own. I loved having Patrick to myself, but it would have been neat to go out on a regular date, like Hallie said.

I made up my mind that next time Patrick came, I'd say I wanted to go to the movies, or to Bondi Beach.

"If that's what you want," said Patrick.

I nearly jumped out of my skin.

"Patrick?" I felt my cheeks getting warm, because I was remembering the last time we'd been together. I looked up into Patrick's face, and wondered if he was remembering too.

"Of course," he said, but I wasn't sure if he was answering what I'd said, or what I'd thought. He quite often did that, I realized.

I wondered if Hallie would think he was cute.

Patrick gave me his half smile, and I noticed he looked tired. "Does it matter what Hallie thinks?"

"Quit doing that," I said. "Can we go somewhere? Now?"

"Don't you want to finish your e-mail?"

I logged out and looked around for Mr. Beck, but he

was in his office. "I'd rather go with you," I said to Patrick, and took his hand.

"We could go back to the garden and eat apples," said Patrick.

"Huh-*uh*. Let's go . . ." I pretended to consider. "Let's go to the movies."

"On a school day?" Patrick's eyebrows climbed.

"You could change it to a weekend." I looked straight at him, because it was the first time I'd said anything like that.

"Not the movies," said Patrick.

"Bondi then?"

Patrick looked less than pleased. "It'll be pretty crowded."

"Good," I said. And I thought, *That's the point.*

I was still holding his hand, but it felt stiff and kind of cold in mine. I was suddenly afraid he'd make an excuse to let go. Then I thought, *Why should I be afraid? Don't I get any say in this relationship?* And I followed him out of the library.

We hit the beach right away. There were tourists lying on towels and some bikini queens picking their way along the sand. There were moms with little kids, an old guy with a metal detector, and some young guys kicking a ball. There were a few couples (and I bet some of them were skipping class) kissing as if they were alone.

"So, what would you like to do?" asked Patrick. "Do you want to go wading?"

I looked at the foamy waves, all covered in froth. It was hot, and the sun was glaring off of the sand, but I thought about putting my school socks back on over sandy feet and shook my head no.

121

"We could sit on the sand," I said.

Patrick sat down, and let go of my hand so he could hug his legs. It was like he was turning in on himself.

I watched the waves coming in, and tried to find a smooth patch of sand with my eyes, but there were people every few feet. A little kid dropped his ice cream cone and started bawling, and his mom said to shut up, or she'd give him something to cry about.

A guy walked down to the sea and waded in up to his knees. He was kind of chubby, and when he turned sideways I could see he had a big hairy belly. His shoulders were pink, but his chest was pasty white.

"Yech," I said.

Patrick turned to look at me. "Why?"

"Just yech." I twitched my shoulders. "Who could stand to look like that? Or like that woman, either." I pointed to a woman in one of those shapeless dresses that tie at the neck with a bow. Her ankles ballooned over her shoes, and her hair needed washing.

Patrick looked at them. "The bloke's having a great time," he said. "This is the treat he's promised himself all winter. The woman is probably more worried about her aching ankles than her fashion sense."

"But how could she get like that?" I said. "Mom would die first."

"You won't ever look like that," said Patrick. He switched his attention back to me, and seemed to be looking at me feature by feature. "You'll stay cute for a couple of years more at least." The way he said it didn't seem like he was paying me a compliment.

"You think I'm cute?"

"Aren't you?" Patrick pressed the tip of my nose

gently with one finger. "Little nose, dimples, big brown eyes. That makes cute, doesn't it?"

"I guess." I looked into his eyes. He smiled.

"What's the problem, Rowena? You're cute, but that's not why I like to look at you."

"Say what? You're kind of losing me."

"You're *real*," said Patrick. He ran one finger down my cheek and flipped my hair. "You can walk through a bush or get blown about by the wind, get caught out in the rain . . . and you still come out of it looking the same. That's what I love about you."

I guess I went on staring at him, but he got up and hoisted me onto my feet. He'd just said he loved me . . . kind of . . . but the way he pulled me up was nothing special.

"Does that mean you don't like it if I wear makeup?" I asked.

"Wear what you like," said Patrick. "You'll still be the same you underneath it, unless . . ." He stopped, and I wondered if I was in for another disappearing act.

"Unless *what?*" I said.

"Oh, unless you judge too much."

We walked along the sand, zigzagging between kids and couples and tottering sandcastles. I was trying to enjoy the famous Bondi Beach, but things seemed out of synch. A few people glanced at us, but no one showed any interest. Patrick answered when I said something, but he didn't talk much otherwise. I got the feeling he was thinking of something else.

"I guess I'll go back," I said. "There's not much point in this."

"Would you rather be doing that?" asked Patrick.

He nodded toward a couple kissing on the sand. They were all wound up in a towel.

"Not like *that*," I said. My voice sounded kind of tight.

"No, not like that," said Patrick, more gently.

The ball the guys had been kicking landed right in front of us, and Patrick gave it a neat punt with his foot. He punted again, and intercepted it when it bounced back from a pile of sand. His next kick sent it back among the other guys, who kicked it back. Patrick caught it, and seemed to blend in with the group. I could see five or six boys, all wearing pants and tees or polos. They were horsing about, and calling one another in foghorn voices. One was Patrick, but I couldn't tell which.

"Patrick!" I called. "I've gotta go."

"Better push off then, darling," said a boy with a tat. I knew *that* wasn't Patrick.

Another made a kissing sound. "Or you could come and have a drink with me. . . ."

A tall boy gave him a shove on the shoulder. "You find your own girl, OK?"

"OK, OK. Keep your hair on."

Tats winked at me, and flicked me a wave.

"He thinks you're cute too," said Patrick, coming up beside me. "You'd better shake some of that sand off." He brushed me down, just like Hallie or Mom might have, then gave me a peck on the cheek. "Catch you later, Ro."

"When?" I asked, but my next step took me into the library at Clancy High.

"When what?" asked Mr. Beck, who was shelving

books with a steady clopping sound. "Have you logged off that computer, Rowena?"

I looked up at the clock, and there was still half an hour of lunchtime to go. "Is it OK if I carry on?" I asked.

"If no one else has booked it," said Mr. Beck.

I logged back in, and started to answer Hallie's e-mail.

>*Neat! You're on e-mail . . . zat a school addy?*
Yo. Mr. Beck (the library teacher) set it up for me.
>*What the heck kind of name is OSYTOVL?*
It was a typo, is all. He's just a regular guy.
>*And how come you were off in a rose garden,*
>*anyways? Where was your mom while this was*
>*going on?*
Mom's in Melbourne. I've got a sitter, would you believe? Mom wouldn't let me stay alone. Want to come move in with me?
>*Did you cut class? Seems this guy is always taking*
>*you off alone. Don't you guys ever go to the*
>*movies or eat at Greedy Gus like a regular cou-*
>*ple?*
Sure we do. We went to Bondi at lunch today and he kicked a ball about with some other guys. <g> He says he loves that other guys think I'm cute.
C-ya. Ro.

Hallie e-mailed me maybe twice each week.

I told her about my times with Patrick, but I kind of adjusted them, so they sounded like regular dates. I even found a way to get around the key lock on typing in Patrick's name. It was easy. I just shortened it to Rick. That way I could make believe I was writing about someone else.

Now and again I got a twinge of guilt about what I was doing, but then I'd tell myself it was Patrick's fault for slapping the lip-zip on me in the first place. I had to tell Hallie *something*, and this way I could stick pretty close to the truth.

One problem was that Hallie kept bugging me for a picture of Rick. I put her off once by saying I couldn't get my hands on a digi-cam, but she came back at me saying Rick must have some friends who had one. If I could have gotten ahold of one, I might have snapped some surfer just to get her off of my case. I really wanted a pic of Patrick, but if the guy wouldn't let me recall his face between one date and another, he wasn't going to let me have a photograph. All I had were the odds and ends he'd given me. I didn't tell Hallie about them, except for the rose.

Mom came back, and sat right down with a stack of printouts.

"What's all that, Mom?" I asked. I started reading one upside down. "John Smith. Background. Subject d.o.b."

Mom twitched the paper away from me.

"Who calls their kid John Smith?"

"No one, in this case," said Mom. "All the case studies are assigned pseudonyms for reasons of privacy."

"Yech," I said. "I would hate to be a case study, Mom."

"You're never going to be," Mom pointed out. "You're too darned . . ."

"Well-adjusted." I smirked, blew on my nails, and pretended to polish them on my new JUST KISSABLE tank.

"I don't know about *that*," said Mom darkly, staring at my top. "If being 'just kissable' is the height to which you aspire, it's no wonder you're . . ."

"Normal," I put in. I'm not always so smart-mouthed, but Mom's meaningful pauses were ticking me off.

"Unambitious, I was about to say," said Mom. "Listen up, honey. You can be whatever you want to be, and what do you choose to be? Kissable?"

"Where did that come from? And for your information, Mom, I can't be whatever I want to be. No one can."

"Not without some honest effort, certainly," said Mom.

"No amount of effort will make me good at math," I pointed out. "Last year I had to work my butt off to get a B average. I could never get the grades to be a research chemist. And are you saying I could win *American Idol* with honest effort?"

"You're being silly, Rowena," snapped Mom. "Though a little more work might not go astray. If you spent less time calling Hallie and more doing your assignments—"

"Hallie has an A average," I said coldly.

I could feel a kind of tight feeling around my eyes. I know I should quit, but then I thought, *Why should I quit when I'm right and Mom's unreasonable?*

Then I thought, *Because Mom's the one with the grounding capability,* so I did.

127

Mom didn't quit. She said there I was, then—what more proof did I need? I really had to get out of Hallie's shadow and realize my true potential.

I was so mad at her I was ready to throw her notebook out the window.

Instead, I got ahold of myself and left.

We made up, of course, but it was a real shame we had that spat. It only made things more difficult later on. Mom had to go away again on March 16, and that was when Hallie *really* screwed things up.

- 15 -

UP IN THE CLOUDS.

At one A.M. on March 17 my cell phone danced a little jig on the nightstand.

I cranked my eyes open and blinked in the dim light coming from the clock radio. I couldn't believe anyone would text me at this hour.

The cell phone danced again at five after one.

"All right, already!" My mouth was dry as cotton balls. I worked my jaws a bit, then reached for the cell.

I didn't recognize the number on the display.

Patrick? Sure, he'd said I couldn't text *him*, but maybe he could text *me*?

Dream on, Ro.

I clicked on read.

4got 2 say air ticket Easter vacation. ☺ *H.*

It wasn't from Patrick. The disappointment hit me like a fist.

Then my dozy brain realized that "H" was Hallie. Hallie'd gotten a cell phone?

129

The text she'd sent five minutes ago was longer, so I scrolled on down.

Ro, guess what! Mom's 1 a trip 4 2 2 nz she sez I can come.
I'm stoked guess what nz is next door australia!
C U soon can't wait meet Rick. Has he got a brother? Call me ☺ H.

"Huh?" I said. I bunched my pillow up behind my back and scrolled through the message again. Then I read the second one. When I put them in the right order, they added up to News with a capital N.

Hallie was coming down under at Easter.

I read the messages a third time. I didn't know what to think. Hallie was coming for Easter? When we were little kids, we used to buy cream eggs and make fluffy chicks for our barrettes, and Easter is still kind of fun. What's not to like about a time when it's practically law that you eat chocolate?

Call me, Hallie had written.

OK, I thought. *I will.*

Mom wasn't there to tell me to wait until morning, and Sorrel wouldn't care if I talked on my cell phone all night. I counted back and concluded it was around quarter after eight in Woodbrock. I hit reply and then call, and one ring later Hallie picked up, and squealed a Hallie-style greeting. She must have been just waiting for me to call.

"Ro? Did you get my message? Guess so, or else you wouldn't have called me." Her voice sounded like it would fizz over any minute.

"You got a cell phone?" I asked.

"I should be so lucky! This is Mom's. But Ro, I'll be with you at Easter vacation. Don't you get it? Isn't that just so, so neat?"

"Neat," I agreed.

"You don't sound stoked," said Hallie reproachfully. "Here's me doing the happy dance and you just say, 'Neat.' "

"I'm trying not to wake Sorrel," I said. "It's one A.M., Hallie."

Hallie yelped. "Who's Sorrel? You'd better not like her better than me. You never mentioned *her* in your e-mails!"

"She's just—"

"I thought it was, like, suppertime or something. Gotta go, Ro—Mom's giving me daggers, 'cause Beth Anne's mom is carpooling today. But listen up, I'll see you at Easter, OK? And we'll hit the chocolate trail."

"No—Hallie, wait! Is this, like, settled?" I asked. "Do I tell Mom about it and make plans, or is it just something that *might* happen, maybe?"

"Mom's locked in with her time off work," said Hallie. "She sure thinks it's settled."

"But the trip is to New Zealand. New Zealand isn't in Australia."

"It's just next door. What's up? Anyone'd think you didn't *want* to see your best buddy."

"Of *course* I do. I just want to be sure it's really going to happen before I let myself get wired. You know how I hate to get disappointed."

"Trust me," said Hallie. "I'll get there if I gotta catch a ride with a whale. Hallie Thomas is hitting Sydney! All *right,* Mom, I'm hanging up. This is me hanging up—see ya, Ro!"

The call cut off, and the quiet came back. I tried to text Mom, but there wasn't enough credit. Guess I was lucky the call didn't drop out while I was talking to Hallie. Or did I mean while Hallie was talking to me?

I thought about Hallie, my best friend since diaper days, arriving at Sydney Airport. We'd do the sights, but how would she fit in? Hallie Thomas might be ready for Sydney, but was Sydney ready for Hallie? And what would Mom say when I told her Hallie was vacationing with us? She already seemed fairly down on Hallie whenever I mentioned her.

And what about Patrick?

I couldn't sleep. I kept coming up with new scenarios.

Hallie would expect to come out with me and Patrick, but she'd never keep her mouth from motoring off when she did. She'd want to know how, and why, and where, and Patrick would go all cold and distant. Hallie would dis him to me and I'd have to pick sides.

Old buddy or new boyfriend? The advice columns are pretty clear on that subject, but Patrick wasn't a regular boyfriend. There might be "plenty of other fish in the sea," but I laid big odds there wasn't another fish like Patrick in any sea.

Best to keep him and Hallie apart, but I didn't fool myself. Hallie already knew about Patrick, and Patrick . . .

Did Patrick know about Hallie? Of course he did. He'd walked in on our conversation in the janitor's shed at school. He knew about Hallie, but he'd never asked about her. I'd have to kind of warn him. . . .

"Oh, Patrick!" I said aloud. I sometimes did say it when I was alone, just to prove I could. The raspberry Jell-O effect never seemed to snap in when I was by myself.

"Sure, top o' the mornin' to ye!" said a voice outside my window.

I hit the floor of the bedroom with such a thud it might have woken the dead. It didn't wake Sorrel, though. Nothing except the alarm clock ever woke Sorrel.

"Patrick?" I pressed my face up against the security mesh of the window.

"Sure, and who else would it be, me darlin'?"

I could see him now, standing on the path, laughing up at me.

"And will ye not be comin' out to tread the dawn wi' me?"

By now I was laughing too, only I was kind of exasperated underneath. My baby-doll pajamas were in the laundry and I'd gone to bed in panties and a faded T-shirt of Mom's. Just for once, it would have been nice to know when Patrick was coming, and to primp a bit beforehand. He didn't seem to care what I wore, but a girl has her pride.

I pulled on a skirt and a light sweater, splashed my face, and drank a glass of juice to wake myself up. Then I went out to the garden. Patrick grabbed me in his arms and swung me off of my feet.

"*Patrick!*" I couldn't help laughing as he kissed me hard, then set me down.

"Sure, and ye do be all wet!" he said. "Is it washin' your face in the dew ye'll be doin', me darlin'?"

"I washed my face, is all. If you come calling in the middle of the night, what do you expect? And why are you talking weird?"

"Sure, and it's Saint Patrick's Day, me darlin'. 'Tis a sorry spalpeen cannot be putting on his brogue for the girleen of his dreams. . . ." Patrick stopped. "You get the picture?" he said in his ordinary voice.

"I guess I do," I said. "Where did you say we were going?"

Patrick walked me right out the gate and into a thick fog that smelled of grass and juicy green leaves and just a smidgen of mud.

I stopped, because no way could I see where I was going. "Where are we?"

"Sure, where would we be but in a bit o' soft weather, suited to the shores of old Erin?"

"And you're Saint Patrick, right? And you're going to chase away the snakes?"

"That's your job, Ro," said Patrick. He held out his arms. "Jump."

"Jump what? Where?"

Patrick sighed, making the fog quiver. "Ro, just trust me and jump, OK? We're walking through fog and I want you to feel safe."

"OK," I said, and jumped. Patrick caught me, and I put one arm around his neck to anchor myself. I imagined I could hear his backbone creaking with the strain. OK, so I weigh 114 pounds, but that's enough to make backbones creak. I've picked up Hallie, and I *know*.

"You're not heavy, Ro," said Patrick in my ear. He started walking.

"Where are we?" I asked again, because I could feel he was stepping up, as if he were climbing a staircase.

"We're going up to where the fog's not so heavy. How else would we be seein' the sunrise in?"

"Is that what we're doing?"

"Begorrah, the girleen is full of questions! What else? And now you can walk the rest of the way." He dumped me on the ground, took my hand, and led me up a gentle slope. The fog muffled sound, and we might have been walking on thick carpet.

It was kind of claustrophobic, the way the fog tucked itself around me. I could feel it beading on my skin and dampening my hair into curls. I closed my eyes to see if it made any difference, and the gray blankness went dark.

"Here we are," said Patrick.

"No, we're not." I stared into the grayness. And then I saw it thin out like torn cobwebs as each step took me higher.

"Sit down." I could see Patrick quite clearly now in the pearly light. The stars had faded and there was a streak of paler color in the sky. He was knee-deep in the fog, so it looked as if he were wading in oatmeal. He folded himself down and the fog lapped up to his waist.

"You could be a merman," I said.

Patrick sighed. "Sure, darlin', I can niver be seein' why ye do be wantin' me to be special, loike. . . ."

"You *are* special," I pointed out. "Now stop talking Irish. Is it dry enough to sit on that grass?"

"Grass?"

"That grass you're sitting on, is it dry? Oh, never

mind." I hunkered down and dipped my hand in the fog to check for myself. My nose nearly dipped in too as Patrick pulled me onto his lap.

"Sit here, Ro. You know *I'm* dry."

I snuggled up to him. "What are we waiting for?"

"Sunrise." Patrick blew my hair away from his face and I felt him rest his chin on my shoulder. "Bring it on," he said, and almost right away the light streak in the sky turned from ghost gray to the palest blue-green ever. Streaks of pink followed, blending until the whole eastern sky looked like mother-of-pearl. It was so beautiful I could feel my heart thudding against my ribs.

The light grew, and then two shafts of gold shot down like spotlights.

"They call it the Eyes of God."

I felt a long shiver go down my back when Patrick said that.

"Patrick . . ." I said.

"Yes?" Patrick's arms tightened around me, and I felt him kiss my cheek.

"You're not . . . an angel, are you?"

There was a silence while Patrick watched the sunrise, and I waited for him to answer. Then the sun came up in a hard rim of gold like a giant's dollar, and I saw the landscape spread below us, green as emeralds. I think I gasped, because the landscape really was below . . . hundreds of feet below.

We were sitting in the clouds.

"You are a *jerk,* Patrick Carroll," I said when I got my breath back.

"Don't you like it?"

"How do we get down?"

I felt Patrick shrug. "We walk. The same way we get back from anywhere."

"We walk." My voice sounded kind of hollow.

"You haven't minded before."

"We haven't gone hiking through the clouds before!"

I scrambled out of Patrick's lap and stared at him. My stomach gave a sudden gurgle, and it sounded so comical I laughed.

"Breakfast," said Patrick.

I closed my eyes as we walked down through the clouds. Call me a coward but I did not want to see what my feet were doing. I wasn't surprised when I opened my eyes and saw where he'd brought me for breakfast. I'd been smelling roses quite a while.

We were back in Saint Valentine's Garden.

There was dew on the grass, but what's a bit of dew to a girl who's just walked in the clouds? I sat on down and grabbed two handfuls of good green grass. A few petals drifted down, and I looked up at a bunch of big roses colored with pink and yellow all mixed together. They looked like the sunrise I'd just watched.

"This is a Peace rose," said Patrick, picking one.

"Okaaay." I took it in my hand. "Patrick, you are a . . ."

"Jerk," he said sadly, then grinned. "Sure, me darlin', I know. And another thing I know: I'm not an angel."

- 16 -

LITTLE TROUBLES.

Mom was not delighted with Hallie's plans for Easter vacation.

"It was thoughtless of you, Rowena," she said when I called her on the house phone that night. "You knew I had plans for those two weeks."

"You didn't tell me *what* plans," I said.

"Two weeks in Tasmania."

"Even so, how could I have said she couldn't come? Her mom said OK."

"I'm surprised at Grace Thomas, involving us without consulting with me first," said Mom. I could hear her biting off the words, and I felt like hanging up.

I gritted my teeth. "She won a competition, Mom! Was she supposed to consult with you before she entered it?"

"Don't get fresh with me!"

Mom really did say that. Can you believe it? I was surprised she didn't add "young lady!" for extra credit.

"Listen up, Mom," I said. "I was trying to explain."

"Explain," said Mom. "And while you're at it,

138

explain to me why you are using the house phone and not your cell?"

"I kind of ran out of credit while I was calling—"

"Hallie," said Mom. "And Hallie didn't call you because . . . ?"

"She texted me. I called her." I didn't tell Mom it had been the middle of the night. "Hallie's mom won this contest. You know she enters fifty squillion contests a year. She had to take the trip when the rules said, and the trip was for two people, so of course she's bringing Hallie."

"Of course," said Mom dryly. "And of course Hallie thinks it an easy matter to take a hop, skip, and jump over the Tasman Sea. And of course you think it will be way cool to have her come visit you here."

"Her mom agreed," I said.

"Obviously." Mom sounded kind of grim. "I guess Grace will contact me *before* Hallie arrives on our doorstep?"

"I guess," I said. "Or you could call her."

"I could," said Mom, "but don't you think it's her responsibility?" Mom must have recalled we were having an interstate conversation landline to cell phone, because she said, "We'll discuss this later, Rowena," and ended the call.

She did not call me "honey."

Mom had simmered down by the time she came back to Sydney. She'd managed to change our bookings over to the winter vacation, and Hallie's mom had sent her a long e-mail explaining the whole plan. "Grace has booked a two-week tour of the islands," explained Mom. "There's a stopover in Sydney, and Hallie will fly on later and meet up with her mom at the end of the tour."

"Neat!" I said.

Mom still wasn't calling me "honey." "Listen up, Rowena," she said, while we were eating dinner. "If Hallie comes to stay over, there need to be some ground rules."

"Hallie can look after herself," I said.

"I'm sure she can," said Mom, "but I am not negotiating with you every single day."

"She might as well not come if we can't do anything," I said. I tried to sound reasonable, but it came out a little snippy.

"That's your problem, Rowena," said Mom. "And if that little trouble is the worst you ever face, you will be exceedingly fortunate."

Maybe I didn't look convinced, because she said, "If you had troubles like some of the kids in my case notes . . ."

I sighed. I recalled that when I was a little tyke, Grandpa Maven used to tell me to eat my broccoli because the children in Somalia were starving. That didn't make me like broccoli. There was broccoli on my plate today. Some things never change.

"Take Jane Jones. She's had meningitis and lost the use of both hands and one leg," said Mom. "John Smith was bashed by a gang of hoodlums on his way home from a dance. His girlfriend was killed. Tom Green has fetal alcohol syndrome. He's nine. On good days he can count to three. And you think *you're*—"

"All right, already!" I pushed my plate away.

Mom sighed. "I'm sorry, honey. I guess I spend so

much time studying kids with major problems that things get a little out of perspective." She got up and gave me a hug. "Guess I forget to count my blessings, too."

"Like, we're not in the Roach Hotel?" I said.

"Like, I've got a good, normal-type kid."

I was glad Mom was back in Mom mode again, but I wondered what she'd say if she knew her "normal" kid had spent Saint Patrick's Day morning sitting in the clouds.

The next day, I went to the library before class and wrote Hallie an e-mail.

Mom's been laying down rules. You know the deal. No staying out past nine on a school night. No guys in the house unless she's home.
Easter vacation is mid-April through May first. How does that fit in with your mom's dates? If you're here during the semester, you'll just have to entertain yourself all day.
C-ya, Ro.

Hallie e-mailed me back right away.

Mom's tour starts April 14, but we hit Sydney on the twelfth. Yay! Hope you got plenty of fun stuff planned. I had to hock birthday presents for the next five years to get Mom to say yes!☹
Mom goes, "Wouldn't you like to see New Zealand, Mahalia?"
I go, "I'd rather see Ro."

Mom goes, "You can see Rowena when she gets home."
I go, "I'd rather see Ro than see New Zealand."
I kind of wore her down and she gave in.
>you'll just have to entertain yourself all day.
Sure. <vbg> I'll let Rick entertain me.
C-ya soon, H. ☺
P.S. I'm gonna pack my swimsuit. You gonna take me to that Rockslide place? & that rose garden?
P.S. again. You still haven't sent me any pix . . . or said if Rick's got a brother.

I wrote Hallie again at lunchtime.

>I kind of wore her down and she gave in.
That's the Hallie we all know and love.
>you'll just have to entertain yourself all day.
>Sure. <vbg> I'll let Rick entertain me.
He's pretty busy.

After I wrote that, I stared at the cursor for a while. *Flick. Flick. Flick. Flick.* I found I was blinking in time with it, and looked away before I got hypnotized. I had a kind of hollow feeling about Patrick and Hallie.

If I kept making excuses for them not to meet, Hallie was going to think I was jealous, or had gotten antsy in case she stole my boyfriend.

I felt like bumping my forehead against the computer desk. No matter which way I looked, this situation wasn't pretty. If the two of them got together, Hallie would mouth off and Patrick would go remote. If I kept them apart, Hallie would despise me. And you know what was *really* making me antsy? She'd be right.

I didn't want Hallie along on our dates. She'd think they were weird. She'd think Patrick was weird.

She'd be right about that, too.

And maybe Patrick wouldn't go remote. Maybe he'd like her too much. Guys do like Hallie. They like her hundred-watt smile. Hallie never had trouble finding a partner for "Spin the Bottle" . . . until she and little old Tedson had their gridlock.

I groaned, and Mr. Beck looked at me kind of funny. I started typing again.

He might be away during vacation, but I hope not. I really want you two to meet.

I logged out. The only place I could think of to be alone was the janitor's shed, so I went and sat on the coil of twine. I really needed to talk to someone.

"Will I do?" asked Patrick.

He was leaning on the wall, looking down at me.

"You're a part of the trouble!"

"Only a part? That makes a change."

"Say what?"

"Usually I'm the *whole* trouble."

"Whose?" I asked suspiciously.

"Mine." He looked kind of pale, or maybe it was the light in the janitor's shed.

"He's a groundsman," said Patrick.

"Quit that," I said.

Patrick hunkered down and took hold of my hands. He was looking right into my eyes. "I don't want to be any trouble to you, Ro." There was something in his eyes that turned my stomach to mush. "Would you rather I didn't come?"

I was about to snap at him for pulling out the same old line again when I realized he meant it. He was offering to get out of my life if that would solve my little troubles.

"No!" I said. I held on to his hands. "I want you here . . . only . . ."

"Real life gets in the way," said Patrick sadly. Then he gave that cute half smile. "You want to go sit in a snow cave?"

"What's a snow cave?" I was still gripping his hands. I loved how they were bigger and warmer than mine.

"You ever see a fall of snow that no one has walked on?" asked Patrick.

"No. It's mostly kind of cruddy."

"The snow falls on the trees and bends the branches down, and pretty soon they touch the ground. Underneath there's a snow cave."

"Brrrr," I said.

"We could walk in the clouds again," said Patrick.

"I . . ."

"Not today, then." Patrick let go of my hands, then leaned in and kissed me gently. He had his fingers tangled in my hair, but I scarcely noticed the tug. I would have gone with him anywhere. Patrick pulled back, then kissed the tip of my nose. "Love you, Ro," he said, and then he was gone.

I stayed in the shed until the music played for the end of lunch. I felt like cutting class, but Mom and I had only just gotten civil again. I sat in Music Theory wishing I'd gone with Patrick. I felt kind of weird and wistful, like I knew I wouldn't be walking on clouds again.

17

MR. NOBODY?

Hallie was first off the airplane. She came bobbing through the gate lounge, talking up a storm with a tall blond guy. He was laughing, and Hallie flashed her million-dollar smile and tossed her braids. I heard them patter on her hot-pink JUST KISSABLE tank.

"Snap!" I said, and jerked my thumb at my own chest.

Hallie dropped her carry-on bag at the blond guy's feet and flung her arms around me. "Ro! Buddy!"

"Hiya, Hallie." I could feel a grin stretching my mouth. It was so darned good to see her. "Where's your mom?"

"Somewhere." Hallie turned back and waved, and I saw Ms. Thomas. "Go get a coffee, Mom. Your next flight is forty-five minutes away."

"Thank you, Mahalia," said Ms. Thomas, grinning. "I never knew that." She turned the grin on me. "Hiya, Rowena." Then she glared at Hallie. "You behave, Mahalia, or you're toast. Damn! I'm whacked." She went off to find that coffee.

"You tired?" I asked.

145

"I slept ten hours. So where's Rick? Did he go away already?"

Hallie had handed me a get-out-of-jail-free card, and I blew it. Instead of giving her a casual "yeah," I stammered something about not being sure.

"You're *not sure* if your guy's away?" yelped Hallie. "You're kidding me, right?"

"He said he might be around." That sounded lame, but at least it was true.

Hallie rolled her eyes and flung out her hands. I cringed. I'd kind of forgotten how in-your-face Hallie can be. "Looks like I've gotten here just in time," she said. "You've been letting that dirtbag jerk you around."

I picked up Hallie's carry-on bag. "Let's go get your baggage."

"This is it," said Hallie. "You and I have got some serious stores to hit. How do we get to your place? And guess what—Pop got me a cell phone that takes pics! Is that cool, or what? And Mom gave me a guidebook full of cool places in Oz."

I'd been kind of stunned by my first sight of Australia, but Hallie bounced along the concourse to the rail platform like she'd been doing it every week of her life. I bought us both tickets, and we got on the train.

"This is neat." Hallie flipped the seat over so we could sit facing each other. "How's your mom? Still mad at me?"

I got a twinge of unease. "She was surprised, is all. You don't expect people to win trips to New Zealand."

"You don't expect people to come to Australia for a year either," said Hallie.

The train swooped into Central and I got us onto the North Shore line.

"You really know your way around," said Hallie. "Whoa—whoa, Nellie! Will you look at *that?*"

That was a dark boy with enormous dark eyes. He was wearing a tight white tank that showed every muscle.

"Man! I want a slice of that!" Hallie made bug eyes. "And hey—there's one for you!"

The red-haired boy next to the dark boy turned around and stared at Hallie. A twinge of recognition went through me, and I kind of half raised my hand.

Patrick?

The redhead gave me a *do I know you?* look, then smiled and pointed to the seat opposite. "Want to sit with us, Rena?"

I shook my head no, and said, "We get off next stop."

"You know that guy?" Hallie asked as we exited the train at Clancy Station.

"Kind of . . ." I replayed the guy's face. "Yeah, his name's Tim. He was at a college Mom took me to for work, and I've met him a couple times since."

"He a friend of Rick's?"

I shook my head. "Let's split. Mom will be waiting."

Mom sighed when she took in our identical shirts.

"Coincidence, huh, Mom?" I said. "They've got the same shirts back home."

"So I see," said Mom dryly.

Hallie giggled. "That guy on the airplane copped a good eyeful. He asked was it a description or, like, an invitation."

147

"Come on," I said quickly. "Put your bag in my room."

"You can go in the spare if you'd rather," Mom suggested, but Hallie said no, that we had a lot of catching up to do.

"I guess that means you'll be talking half the night," said Mom.

"No, Doc," said Hallie. "We'll prolly talk *all* night."

Mom groaned. "Just keep it down, OK? Oh, and Ro, will you feed the birds?"

"What bird?" asked Hallie. "You got a little old canary in a cage?"

"No, but the guy who owns this place has two galahs," I said. "Come and see."

I filled the hopper up with seed from the store in the pantry, and topped up the water bowl. The galahs came down to watch.

Hallie giggled. "They sure are cute little guys, Ro! They just about match our shirts."

One of the galahs made a *grrrrk*? noise, and Hallie laughed some more. She seemed to be bubbling over with things she wanted to see and do. "So," she said as we came back into the kitchen with the empty seed can. "We gonna hit the beach right now, or wait for Rick to show?"

"Who's Rick?" asked Mom.

I saw Hallie's astonished face, but she made a quick recovery.

"What was his name? The guy on the train. He was sitting with his yummy buddy. You said your mom knew him?"

"You mean *Tim*," I said, a bit too loudly. I felt my cheeks making like a tomato.

"Tim?" Mom gave me a kind of quizzical look.

"The redheaded guy from that college."

Mom's face cleared. "That's right. Nice boy. You've been seeing him?" She looked a little too interested.

"Now and then," I said. "He's Claire's cousin."

"He was with a friend, you say?"

Hallie giggled. "Sure was. Dark hair, kind of Latino. *Yum!*"

"Oh." Mom lost interest.

"So," said Hallie. "We gonna hit the beach?"

On the way to the station, I took a detour to show Hallie Clancy Park. I was kind of hoping Patrick might be there.

"Where's your school?" asked Hallie. "I want to see the janitor's shed." She giggled. "The place you and Rick make out."

"It's just a shed," I said. "I'll show you later."

"Awww . . ."

"You want to go to the beach before dark?"

We ran back to the station. Hallie's cornrow braids bounced, and a few people stared. You don't see many cornrow braids around Clancy.

Twenty minutes later we got off of the train at Bondi Junction and made our way to the beach. Hallie peered around hopefully.

"Where're the hunks?"

"It's a Tuesday," I said. "And besides, it's fall. There were more people here when I came before."

"When you cut classes to go out with Rick?"

"I never cut classes," I said.

"Well, excuse me!"

"I don't. I'd be toast if Mom found out, and she's got a spy on the staff. Claire Tilley's mom."

There was a nasty silence; then Hallie said, "You don't have to lie to me."

"I'm not."

Hallie wheeled and eyeballed me. "You said you and Rick came here on a date during the school lunch hour."

"So?" *Oh, darn it,* I thought as I saw where Hallie was going with this. Why did she have to have an elephant's memory?

"It took us a half hour to get here from your stop," said Hallie, "so either you've got an extra-long lunch hour, or else your so-called date lasted about two seconds. Seems more likely to me you cut class."

I didn't say a word. There was nothing I *could* say.

Hallie shook her head kind of scornfully. "You didn't want me to come, did you?"

"I did so!" I blurted. "You're my best buddy!"

"That didn't stop you from selling me a load of trash. You haven't got a boyfriend."

I stared at her.

Hallie held out her hand. "Give me your cell phone."

"Where's yours?"

She snapped her fingers and I handed it over. She fiddled with it a bit and got into the phone directory. She started scrolling through the names, reading them aloud. " 'Mom, Claire, Cam the Man, Tai . . . ' " She looked up. "So where's Rick's number? Come on, Ro . . . you telling me you haven't got your boyfriend's number in your cell?"

"He doesn't have one," I said.

"House phone?"

"He doesn't . . ."

"Yeah? And he doesn't have a camera? And your mom doesn't know he exists?"

I didn't answer.

"I asked about Rick and she was, like, 'Who's he?' "

"Rick's not his real name," I said. "It's kind of a . . ." I recalled what Mom had said about her case histories ". . . a pseudonym."

"So what's his real name, then?" Hallie clicked her fingers. "C'mon, Ro, *dish!* Either the guy doesn't exist, or else he's bad, bad news."

I made a big effort. I really did. "It's P . . . P . . . Oh!" The lip-zip was hard in place.

Hallie was quivering her head like a rattler giving a warning. "I don't *believe* you, Ro! I always thought you were the one person I could rely on to be straight with me, and now you go do this!" Then suddenly she shrugged, and tossed my cell in the air. She caught it again, handed it over, and laughed. "Oh, well. It means we can hunt us some hunks without Mr. Nobody getting in the way. Wonder where Mr. Train Hunk lives?"

She grinned. Only it wasn't the million-dollar grin I remembered. It wasn't real.

I couldn't be comfortable with Hallie after that. Not with her thinking I was a big liar. I didn't say squat, so Hallie gave up on me and started whistling through her retainers and eyeing up the guys around us.

At dinner she told Mom about the flight, and some of the news from home. She talked to me, too, but I could hardly bring myself to answer. Mom kept giving me little looks, and she had a furrow between her eyebrows.

Mom need not have worried we'd chatter all night. Hallie would've, but I made like I was asleep. I didn't know what to do. I could tell Hallie she was right, I'd been making things up, but that would be a lie. I could pretend everything was peachy, but that would be a lie as well. It would have been better if Hallie had kept on being scornful. Then I could have hated her some.

I wanted to toss and turn, but that would have said I was awake and fretting. . . . At last I must have dozed off, because suddenly it was daylight and I had a headache. My eyes felt really weird.

Mom took one look at me at breakfast and told me to go lie down while she and Hallie went to the grocery store.

I lay there for a while, feeling really low; then I sat up. My head banged. I shook it to see if anything rattled, and the ache came in with a crash. I was feeling sick to my stomach as well, and everything looked blurry. I started to panic.

"You've got a migraine," said Patrick. He was sitting at the foot of my bed.

"Patrick!" I crossed my arms over my chest.

"Don't be silly," said Patrick. "I could see a lot more when you went swimming. You do look rough."

"I feel like crud." My stomach heaved. "I'm going to—" I stumbled out of bed and made for the bathroom, banging into walls.

When I crept back to my room, Patrick was prowling around, picking things up and putting them down. "You kept the stone," he said.

"Quit that," I groaned.

Patrick put down the piece of driftwood. "Migraines are the pits."

"How would you know?"

"My . . . someone I knew used to get them." He came to the bed and bent over.

I groaned again, because I thought he was going to kiss me and I was afraid I'd throw up. Instead he put his fingertips on my forehead and started gently massaging my face and scalp. I closed my eyes, because I didn't want him to see my tears, and after a while the headache started to fade. I could still feel it, but it seemed to be someplace else.

I opened my eyes, and a couple of tears spilled out. "How'd you get in here?" I asked; then I thought, *How stupid. How does Patrick get anywhere?*

"I walked," he said. "Are you feeling better?"

"A little. You know Hallie's here?"

Patrick bent and peeked under the bed. "Where?"

I managed a smile. "Out with Mom. She's mad at me. She thinks I made you up."

Patrick went still. "You *told* her?"

"What do *you* think? That darned lip-zip-trick of yours wouldn't let me, but I kind of said a couple of things, and Hallie . . ."

"Kind of filled in the gaps and joined the dots and made a substance out of a shadow."

"So?" I said.

Patrick shrugged. "So . . . nothing. I'm sorry, Ro, but I did warn you from the start."

"Uh-*uh*," I disagreed. "You just scared the bejesus out of me and then lip-zipped me without a by-your-leave."

153

"I've messed up your life, haven't I?"

I cracked a smile. "What's a bit of a mess between friends?" And I recalled how Grandpa Maven always said you can't bake a cake without cracking eggs.

Patrick laughed. "I've never been called a *cake* before."

I looked around the room. It looked bad, with Hallie's stuff and mine all mussed about. My head felt better, but I was clammy with perspiration. "Patrick . . . would you take me to the garden?"

Patrick held out his hands, and I pulled myself into a sitting position. The room spun, but I got out of bed.

"Better change," said Patrick. "I won't peek." He turned his back.

"You get away from that mirror, Patrick!" I said.

In Saint Valentine's garden, the roses thought it was summer. The bees were humming away, and there were butterflies on the leaves. I lay down and put my head in Patrick's lap. A petal fell onto my cheek, and Patrick stroked it away. Water trickled in the little fountain.

"I feel like I'm in heaven," I said.

Patrick went still. His fingertips were suddenly cold on my face. "Don't say that, Ro. Be careful what you wish for."

When Mom and Hallie came back, I was drinking coffee in the kitchen.

"You look better," said Mom. "I thought you might be coming down with the flu."

"It was a migraine," I said.

"It might have been, I guess. Your father used to get them."

"He *did?*"

"Yes," said Mom in the clipped voice she always uses for that subject. "Usually when he had backed himself into a corner."

"But my head really *hurt!*" I said indignantly.

"So did his. They were perfectly genuine migraines," said Mom. "But like a lot of stress-related illnesses they were symptoms of some underlying inadequacy. In his case, he was escaping the consequences of his actions."

I noted she'd switched to Dr. Maven mode. "You've been reading too many case histories," I said.

Hallie took a shower, then went into my room. She was being tactful—or else avoiding me.

"You can make your bed, since you're recovered," said Mom. "If you have another episode we might need to look at medication."

Hallie was standing with her hands behind her back, eyeballing me when I went into the bedroom. "Hey, Ro."

I mumbled something.

"You been to the store?"

"I've had a migraine," I said.

"Where did these come from?" Hallie whipped her hands forward like a conjurer and showed me a bunch of roses. They weren't the stiff kind you get from the florist, but big open blooms in pinkish yellow.

"Peace," I said.

"Say what?"

"The roses are called 'Peace.' "

"But where did they come from?"

P for Peace, I was thinking. *P for Patrick.*

"They're from him, aren't they?" said Hallie. "Your boyfriend?"

"I thought I'd made him up? You called him Mr. Nobody. Maybe I sent these to myself."

Hallie shook her head. "You'd have made it one red rose. Or at least you'd have made a proper bunch with buds and leaves."

Hallie filled a jug with water, then jammed the roses in. "Peace," she said. "Did you guys have a fight? Is that why he's not been around?"

"He has been around," I pointed out.

Hallie's eyes bugged. "Did he come in *here*? In this room?"

"Yes. But don't make anything of it. I was sick as a dog."

"Pretty cool, with your mom away," said Hallie. She wasn't flashing her retainers and hugging herself or making sassy comments. Instead she was frowning, like some stern ebony goddess statue. "So come on," she said, turning to face me. "What's this guy's real name? *Dish!*"

18

SMITH OR JONES?

Once Hallie gets her teeth into anything, it might as well give up.

"I can't tell you his name," I said for, like, the tenth time.

"But *you* know it."

"I can't tell you. I can't say it."

Hallie clicked her fingers. "Ost-whatever. You can't pronounce it?"

I shrugged. That was close enough.

"What's he look like?"

"Just regular."

"Where's he live?"

"I don't know. Really. Quit hassling me, Hallie!"

"Where do you guys meet?"

"All over. Clancy Park. At school. In the Blue Mountains. Here."

"Sounds like he's stalking you," said Hallie. "You gonna tell your mom?"

"It's not like that. He'd never hurt me."

"Listen up, Ro." Hallie sat on the foot of the bed,

where Patrick had sat. "You've gotta see this guy is playing you for a sucker."

"He's never asked me for anything, or taken anything."

"Yet," said Hallie. "Has he—"

"*No.*"

"But you guys make out?"

"Quit it, Hallie," I said. "It's nothing heavy. How'd you like it if I kept grilling *you* about your love life?"

"I'd think you gave more than a dime about what happens to me," said Hallie. "You're bluffing, Ro. This guy is no good, or else why the big secrets?"

I didn't answer. I couldn't.

"These places he takes you," said Hallie. "Bondi Beach. And what was the other one? Rockslides? And some other beach?"

"Rockslides and Ocean Beach," I snapped. "And Meander. And there was a place called Remarkable Rocks." I wished I'd held my tongue, but it was weird like that. If Patrick used a lip-zip, Hallie seemed to have turned on a faucet.

"All right!" Hallie grabbed up her guidebook off of the nightstand and flipped it open at the back. "Meadowbank, Meadows, Meandarra . . ."

"Quit that," I said.

"Meander, Meatian, Mebul . . . Moe, Morewell." She flipped pages. "Ocean Beach. Rockslides? Nuh-huh. No Remarkable Rocks, either."

"There was a town called Alice Springs. We went to a place near there."

"Private jet?" asked Hallie.

"Say what?"

"There's a place called Alice Springs . . . in the

Northern Territory. I calculate it's around two thousand miles from Sydney. And the only place called Meander is around one thousand miles from here."

I chewed my lip.

"This guy really has sold you a bill of goods," said Hallie flatly.

I stared at her angry face. She was mad as hell, but not at me.

"Listen," I said. "These places we go . . . they're kind of pretend. Like games. He just gives them names for fun."

"You go swimming in a pretend place? You have picnics in pretend gardens?"

"It's a *game*. We walk and he tells me where we are."

"You sit in the janitor's shed and play pretend?"

"He kind of makes me see them," I said. "Like virtual reality."

Hallie grabbed my flip-flops and jammed them into my hands. "Get those on. You and I are going out."

Mom was head-down in her case notes, and never looked up.

"If the doc had any sense, she'd be keeping a better study on *you*," said Hallie.

"You leave Mom out of this."

"Like you have? What's he giving you?"

"I am not doing drugs."

"Like you'd know? Does this guy give you candy? Soda? Ro, he could be spiking it with acid or Rohypnol. . . ."

"He doesn't give me candy! Got that? He gives me *flowers*. He'd never hurt me!"

"Of course not," said Hallie. "He'd only mess with

159

your mind and make you lie to your mom and your friends. I mean, *Rick?*"

"You kept bugging me," I said defensively. "Where are we going?"

"Your school. The park. Where you meet this Mr. Nobody."

Patrick wasn't at the school. Hallie hauled me along every little trail of Clancy Park, but Patrick didn't show. "I gotta get a look at this dirtbag," growled Hallie.

"Well, you won't."

"And you won't either, while I'm around."

I felt like I'd jumped on a freight train and now I couldn't get off. I should *never* have mentioned Patrick to Hallie. I'd gotten around the lip-zip by changing his name, and now I was paying for it.

Hallie stuck to me like a cocklebur. Once, she even followed me into the bathroom.

"You can go out," I said. "He doesn't *do* bathrooms."

"He does bedrooms, though," she said darkly.

I scowled at her. I was maxed out with control freaks. At least Patrick admitted his rules were to protect himself.

"Against what?" asked Hallie when I told her that. "The mob? His supplier? Your mom?"

"It's not *like* that!" I said for the twentieth time.

I longed to see Patrick. I needed to compare him with this monster Hallie had conjured up in his image. I *knew* he wasn't spiking my drinks. If I just got Hallie to *see.*

If Patrick took us both to the Rockslides, or to the Remarkable Rocks . . . or . . . Not to Saint Valentine's

Garden, and not to walk on the clouds. Those were our special places. So was the tree-trunk cave where he'd given me the first missed kisses. And in the garden, the kiss that didn't miss . . .

"Snap out of it!" said Hallie, and jabbed me hard with her elbow. We were in the kitchen, fixing some nachos, and I nearly dropped the can of beans.

"What do I have to do to convince you?" I asked.

Hallie looked at me hard. Then a million-dollar grin spread over her face. The retainers flashed like armor. "What do I have to do to convince *you*? It's him who has to do the convincing," she said.

"How?"

"Make him dish the dirt on why the secrets. And let me look him over."

I thought of Patrick with Hallie, and this horrible red jealous feeling came over me.

He's mine, I thought. And that was when I realized how unhealthy this thing with Patrick really was.

I slung the tray of nachos into the oven.

You were thinking of me, so I came, said Patrick's voice in my head.

Right! I thought. *I'll run a little test.*

I waited until Hallie was taking a shower the next day, and then I went to the park. I sat on the seat near the Fernery, and thought of Patrick.

Pretty soon, Patrick wrapped his arms around my shoulders and brought his cheek against mine. "Your friend gone, Ro?"

"No," I said. "She's taking a shower." For the first time in months I didn't feel happy to see him. I had a kind of heavy feeling in my stomach. "Where were you just now?" I asked.

"Waiting for you."

"But *where*? Were you in the garden? Or out near Alice?"

I felt Patrick sigh against my cheek. My stomach wanted to melt. "I wasn't anywhere special," said Patrick. "I never am, except when I'm with you."

I twisted around and broke his hold. "But *where* were you? Where do you live?"

Patrick got that wary look again.

"You've got some smart tricks, all right," I said. "But you've gotta have a real life somewhere. Everyone has."

"My only life's with you."

That sounded romantic, but I didn't want romance. "Remember Mom?" I said.

He moved his head in a kind of half nod.

"Sure you do. You saw her at the Blue Mountains. If you recall, you said you'd say 'hi' if she did."

"She didn't notice me," said Patrick.

"If she had, would you have said anything?"

"Yes, of course."

"I see," I said. "Well, I gotta get back to Hallie. Thank you for the roses."

I got up and walked away.

It was the first time I had ever left Patrick so abruptly since the time we went west. . . .

Hallie was just about steaming when I got back. "Where have *you* been?"

"Out with Mr. Nobody," I said.

"I told you—"

"I *know* what you told me," I said. "And guess what? I agree. *Not* that he'd ever hurt me, but this secrecy thing is not good." I took a deep breath. "Reckon you could use that cell of yours to take some mug shots?"

Hallie's eyes sparked up. "A stakeout! Wow! When? Where? The park?"

"I guess the best place is where I met him first," I said. "You and I are going to the Roach Hotel."

I couldn't sleep that night, so I went out to the main room. Mom was typing away at her reports. I leaned my chin on her shoulder.

" 'Case fifteen,' " I read aloud. " 'Jack Jones.' "

"Don't do that," said Mom. "These case notes are private."

"Aren't you turning them into a book?"

"Not just as they are," said Mom. "I'm using key characteristics and terms to produce ciphers."

I sighed. "Sure, Dr. Maven. Is this Jack Jones any relation to Jane Jones? The chick with meningitis?"

"No," said Mom. " 'Jones' is the key I'm using for subjects whose educational difficulties stem from a random nontargeted—"

"Whoa!" I said.

Mom glanced up. "Sorry, honey. I mean, the subjects I call Jones all have problems because they've had an unavoidable accident or disease. Get it?"

I did. "The little kid who can't count. He's not a Jones?"

"Fetal alcohol syndrome is a preventable condition," said Mom. "All his mom had to do was stay off the booze for a lousy few months. . . ." She must have seen me staring, because she said, "What?"

"That doesn't sound like you, is all."

163

"I get so *angry*. . . ." Mom sighed. "The 'Greens' all have problems that come from someone else's actions."

"They've got someone to blame, you mean. Go on," I said. Anything to take my mind off of tomorrow's stakeout. I'd already decided it wasn't a good idea.

"The 'Browns' do poorly at school for no apparent reason," said Mom. "They test normal but perform way below par. Or just plain don't like school. And the 'Smiths' have problems they blame *themselves* for."

"And you're doing this for . . . ?"

"I'm doing a study to see which type of problem is the most intractable in the educational platform," said Mom. She caught my eye. "Which sorts are hardest to treat. Is it easier if you can blame someone else rather than fate?"

I started reading off names. " 'Jack Jones, Jane Jones, Mary Jones, Anne Jones. Dave Smith, Carl Smith. John Smith' . . . you mentioned him before. What if you get one that belongs in two places? Like, say, a girl who's gone down a dark alley and gotten mugged? She blames herself for going down the alley, but it's really the mugger's fault. Does that make her a 'Smith-Green'?"

"It doesn't work that way. Even if both those elements are in place, one is always dominant. Why the sudden interest, honey? You've never shown a grain of it before."

I wanted to tell Mom everything, to sit down and ask her where she'd put *me* and my Patrick/Hallie problem. But she wouldn't put me anywhere. None of it had a thing to do with education. I wondered if I was a Smith, because I'd blabbed to Hallie, or a Green, because Patrick was making unreasonable conditions, or even a Jones, because I'd happened to meet Patrick and to have a friend like Hallie whose mom won contests. Or was I a Brown, because I was too dumb to get out of the rain?

Well, all this was going to stop, as of tomorrow.

"Mom," I said, "can I borrow your hands-free recorder? Hallie and I want to tape some stuff. . . ."

19

STAKEOUT AT THE ROACH HOTEL.

I hadn't been back to the Roach Hotel since we'd left it more than three months ago. I remembered wishing then that Hallie were with me to dis the balcony apartments and check out cute boys down under. Well, she was with me now.

It was cooler today, and the sidewalk wasn't sticking to my sneakers.

"This is the place," I said.

Hallie looked up at the Roach Hotel, and hunched into the electric-blue hoodie she was wearing. "You stayed *here?*"

"For three days."

"And this is where Mr. Sleaze hangs out? It figures."

"Hallie, quit it! I met him here, is all. You might as well say *I* hang out here."

"Go find out then," said Hallie, and she gave me a little push. "When you get an eyeball, *if* you get an eyeball, flip me the sig."

I stared at the balcony of the apartment Mom and I had rented. I thought I could see the potted plant in the corner. I tilted my chin and looked at the apartment above.

"I can't just go up," I said. "I haven't got a key."

"We can knock on doors. Take orders for Girl Scout cookies or something."

That was a bad idea, and I knew I'd be grounded for a year if Mom found out. "I'll see if I can find him the regular way," I said quickly.

"Sure. It would help if I knew what he looks like."

"He looks like a regular guy," I said.

Hallie sniffed. "That figures."

I wondered if Hallie would see me talking to Patrick. I wondered what people did see when he and I were out and about. The boys at Bondi had kicked a ball with him. . . .

A rasping noise and a loud whistle from across the road announced a gang of boys going by on in-line skates. One was wearing a cap pulled down low and a backpack on his shoulders. He looked at me, then at Hallie, and kind of nodded.

"Is that him?" asked Hallie.

"I'm not sure. . . ." I slipped my hand into my pocket where Mom's little hands-free was nested.

Two guys skated faster, showing off, and Hallie gave them a slow hand clap.

"Ro? I didn't expect to see you here again." Patrick looped his arm through mine from behind, and dropped a kiss on my head. It felt light as a rose petal, and my stomach did its swoop and swirl routine.

"Patrick!" I hugged his arm. "I forgot to thank you properly for the roses."

167

He smiled down at me. "Did they sort out your problem?"

"Say what?"

"You wanted proof you had a boyfriend."

"Is *that* why you gave them to me?" I felt kind of disappointed.

"I thought of doing a card, too," said Patrick, "but what name could I have used?"

"Your own," I said, a bit sharply.

"I couldn't, you know."

I glanced across at Hallie, but she was talking to the guy in the cap. She started walking toward the Roach Hotel, gesturing and flirting as the guy skated slowly beside her.

I kind of waggled my fingers at her. I hoped she'd gotten the signal.

Patrick was also watching Hallie and the guy. As they came closer, I recognized him as Airhead Claire's cousin, Tim.

Hallie put her hand in the pocket of her hoodie and took out her cell phone. She turned to Tim, and started messing with it.

"What's she up to?" asked Patrick.

"Getting Tim's number, I guess. Or his friend's." My voice sounded tight.

Hallie turned and looked straight at me. She lifted up the cell.

"Who's . . ." Patrick's voice faded out. I looked up at him. I saw him shake his head once or twice. "No. No, *no.*"

"Huh?"

Patrick grabbed my elbow. Next thing, we were in Saint Valentine's Garden.

Well, it was kind of Saint Valentine's Garden, but the roses were all broken down to thorny sticks. The cute fountain was cracked and dry, and there was a smell of mildew and rot.

"Patrick?" I looked up at him and got the shock of my life.

His face, that face I loved but could never remember, was wearing an expression I could never forget. One cheek was striped with marks, as if he'd been lying on something sharp, and his eyes were like chips of blue marble. And his mouth . . .

"*Patrick?*" I said again.

He turned on me furiously, and I saw that his white tee—the one I'd teased him about so often—was crumpled and stained. I took a couple steps backward.

"You set me up." If he'd yelled, it mightn't have been so bad, but he just said it in his ordinary voice. It didn't go with the expression on his face. It didn't go with the ruin of Saint Valentine's Garden.

"Say what?" I fell back a couple more paces. The hands-free felt like a neon brick in my pocket.

"You set me up. That girl had a camera."

"It's only her cell . . . she was getting Tim . . ."

Patrick swore, and I jumped. I'd never heard him do that before.

"Don't do that," he said irritably. "I've told you I won't hurt you. Oh, Ro, you were my only chance. . . . Why couldn't you *trust* me?"

"You don't trust me." I was scared—not of Patrick, but of the way things were falling apart. What if he left me here—

"Don't be so bloody stupid!" snapped Patrick. "Of

course I won't leave you here. Have I ever done *anything* to hurt you?"

"Yes!" I blurted. "You're hurting me now!" I was mad, suddenly, good and mad.

"I can't do this anymore," said Patrick. "I thought I could, but I can't."

"You're a freak! A control freak!" I yelled. "Hallie was right. I wish . . ." My voice was shaking, and I had to swallow and start again. "I wish I'd never met you. I wish you were—"

"Don't say that!" Patrick's voice cracked, and he put his hand across my mouth. I remembered the last time he'd done that. It had been kind of playful, kind of serious, and later he'd kissed me in the cave.

That memory hurt so much I pushed him violently away from me.

Both of us stumbled and I fell backward. I thought I'd land on my butt, but someone grabbed me before I hit the ground.

It was red-haired Tim, and he was red-faced as well. "Watch it!" he said, and pushed me back onto the perpendicular.

Two of the other boys said, "Ooh-ah!"

"That is *so* seventh grade," said Hallie. She grinned at the boys, flashing her million-dollar mouthful. "Well, aren't you heroes gonna give me your numbers?" She looked back at me. "So? Are you gonna look for him, or what?"

"I . . ." I could hear my voice, soggy with tears, and Hallie looked at me properly.

"Ro?"

"Did you see him? Did you get it?"

"When? Where?"

"He was just with me . . . we've been to S—" But I couldn't even tell her where we'd been.

Hallie stared.

"Didn't you see him?" I stammered.

"There was no one with you," said Hallie. "I was watching you the whole time."

"No, you weren't. I saw you. You were with those guys."

"I was watching, like you said."

She hadn't been, but there was no point in arguing. "You had your cell out. You were taking a pic, weren't you?"

"No," said Hallie. "Remember Mr. Yummy off the train? I was getting his number off of Tim." She showed me. "But hey, what about the hands-free? If you were with this guy you should have his voice on that."

I took it out of my pocket, stopped it, and ran it back. Then I set it to play.

". . . you see him? Did you get it?" My own voice sounded shaky.

"Where?" said Hallie's voice.

". . . was just with me . . . we've been to S—"

And so it went on. There was not a word from Patrick. And maybe just as well. When I recalled him saying terrible things in his ordinary voice I shivered.

- 20 -

PHOSPHORESCENCE.

Mom had gotten us chocolate eggs for Easter, and Hallie squealed and gave her a hug. "Thanks, Doc!"

Mom rolled her eyes at me.

"Neat, Mom," I said. My hips could do without the chocolate hit, but the rest of me wanted it, all right.

Patrick didn't send anything. At least, I thought he hadn't, until I saw something gleaming white at me from the drawer where I kept my souvenirs.

It was the kangaroo skull.

I didn't show Hallie. I was having trouble talking to Hallie, too.

"So," she said a few days later. "Looks like this guy of yours has left town."

"Looks like it," I said. "Game over."

"Game over," said Hallie. She looked at me funny, like she thought my brain had left the building. "Thing is, why were we playing it?"

I didn't ask her what she meant by that.

* * *

We took in the sights, the way Mom and I had when we first arrived. One day Hallie and I got on a ferry and went to Taronga Zoo. Tim and his buddy Marius turned up by the crocodile exhibit. I don't think it was coincidence, because Hallie looked pretty smug. She didn't tell me if she'd texted them, and I didn't ask.

I looked for Patrick while we were watching the marmosets and the otters, and when we rode the cable car up the hill, but I didn't think he was there. How could I tell, when I didn't know his face?

I missed him horribly.

On the night before Hallie had to leave, we went to an underage rage at the Blue Light. Somehow I wasn't surprised to see Tim there, helping out with the sound system. He nodded to us across the room; then when the strobe lights got going he came and asked me to dance. I glanced at Hallie, but she was already giving Marius the eye.

"I'm gonna call him," she said, and got out her cell. I saw Marius slap his hand to his pocket, pull out a cell, and look puzzled . . . then Tim started dancing. He's a cruddy dancer, but anything was better than waiting . . . waiting for Patrick to slip his hand in mine or drop a kiss on my nose.

We were dancing under one of the strobe spots and I realized it was phosphorescent. Tim's red hair looked kind of purple, and when he said something his teeth flashed like blue glass. He was wearing a plain white tee with the Northcote College logo, and I thought, *You would.* I tried to tell myself it would be nice to dance in a clinch with Tim the way Cam and Claire were doing, but I couldn't make up my mind to do it. Tim was a nice guy, but he wasn't . . .

P. CARROLL.

Say what?

I blinked at the name that seemed to squiggle before my eyes. The music from Luv'n's latest album was battering against my ears, and the lights were flashing in sync. I saw Hallie had gone off with Marius; they were doing what looked like a samba on the floor.

Tim spun around, kind of like a cat on a griddle.

L. WEBB, I read swirling up his other arm.

Tim brushed his fingertips down my arms and raised his eyebrows.

I came in closer, then looked down at his chest. T. TILLEY. "What's that say on your shirt?" I said in his ear.

Tim's hands were resting nervously on my shoulder blades, and when I spoke, he trod on my toe. "Sorry. My shirt? What about it, Rena?"

"It's got writing on it."

"Oh, yeah. I s'pose it shows up under the strobe."

"What is it?"

Tim looked at me funny. "Some of us went to an art camp back in year ten, and we made sig shirts with phos paint."

"You and . . ." My heart was bumping way too fast. I hoped Tim wouldn't notice.

"Robbo Cash, and Jonno over there, Lachie Webb and Marco . . . why?"

"I was wondering if I knew any of them."

"You know Marco."

"I do?"

Tim glanced over my shoulder. "Looks like your mate knows him pretty well."

"Oh, *Marius,* you mean? Yeah, well . . ." I shrugged. "That's Hallie."

Tim laughed, and his hands settled a bit more firmly. If that had been Patrick, my legs would have turned to mush. I liked Tim, but he might as well have been a friendly horse. "Shame she's going," said Tim. "We could've gone out properly in a foursome . . . if Dr. Maben wouldn't mind?"

"Maven!" I said. "Who else have you got on your shirt?"

Tim put his cheek on my head and slipped his hand up the back of *my* shirt. "Dunno. Can't remember. Petey Carroll and Davo Chong, maybe . . ."

I sighed. "Tim . . . do you mind?"

"What? Oh. Sorry." Tim put his hand back where it belonged.

The next day Hallie and I caught the train to the airport.

"Now if I'd only cracked onto Marius sooner . . ." she said. "Like, that day we saw them on the train . . ." She rolled her eyes. "Oh, well, there's always e-mail. And Marius's got a grandpa in L.A."

"L.A.'s nowhere near Woodbrock," I reminded her.

"So? New Zealand's nowhere near Sydney." She twisted one of her cornrows, and I noticed she had a little heart ring on her pinkie. She gave me a straight look. "Guess you wish I'd never come?"

"Oh, Hallie . . ."

"C'n see why," she said. "Did you pull that Mr. Nobody gag on anyone else back home?"

"I—"

"It's only," she said loudly, "that I want to know what to say."

"Don't say anything," I said.

"Forget it, huh?"

I wished *I* could forget it.

"Well . . . better split," she said. "That's my flight." She hugged me good-bye, and the last I saw of her she was heading through security check. A couple of young black guys followed her, and Hallie turned and flashed her retainers at me. Then she hugged herself and held up two fingers.

I smiled and turned away. I had a kind of empty feeling where my best buddy had been, but now that she was gone I could work things out with Patrick.

Well, I thought I could, but Patrick never showed.

I went back to school at the end of the month to start my second semester at Clancy High. Mom did a bunch of lectures, and collected a bunch more studies for her book. It was a pretty long month. Mom was away a lot, and Sorrel came and slept over. "So how's your boyfriend?" she asked. "Did he give you an Easter egg?"

I shook my head, wincing away from the memory of the kangaroo skull.

"You guys broken up?" asked Sorrel.

"Kind of," I said. "We had trust issues."

"There are always other guys," said Sorrel.

Yes, I thought, *but there's nobody else like Patrick.*

I tried to tell myself I was better off without someone who wouldn't answer any questions, but I remembered the fun we'd had, how his fingers had gone stiff with surprise the first time I held his hand, how he'd helped me to float in the Rockslides pool, and shown me shooting stars and the Eyes of God.

I remembered our Valentine picnic, but the garden was spoiled by the last time I'd seen it, wrecked and ruined like my friendship with Patrick.

My friendship with Hallie wasn't in much better shape.

She'd sent me a couple of e-mails since she'd gotten home, but it wasn't the same.

21

CLOUDS AND WATER.

Second semester finished, and at the end of June we caught the ferry down to Tasmania.

"You can't go to Tassie in winter!" said Claire when she heard. "You'll get icicles on your bits!"

"Rubbish," said Luisa. "It's three or four degrees colder than here, maybe."

Claire turned to me. "Don't you do it, Ro. Tim'll pine away."

"No, he won't," I said. I didn't blush, because there was no need.

I knew Tim liked me. I liked him, too, but our kinds of liking were different.

"Is it because you're going back to the States?" he asked. He'd tried to kiss me after a double feature at the movies, and I'd turned my cheek.

"I was seeing someone," I said. "It went wrong."

"Oh, I see," said Tim. "No worries."

I hoped he did see, because I didn't want anyone else on my conscience.

* * *

And now we're down in Tasmania, just Mom and me. It's a beautiful place, and soooo peaceful.

There's some cool scenery, and too much time to think, so I've been going over the last few months in my mind. I'm kind of wondering what I could have done instead of what I did do.

I could have been honest with Hallie.

There's this boy, I might have said. *He won't let me say his name. . . . He takes me to unreal places.*

But saying that would have been just as bad as what I did say. I should have kept my big mouth shut. What's the point in being honest if no one can believe you?

It's early July, and I haven't seen Patrick since the middle of April. Shouldn't the missing-him pain have faded a bit by now?

I wish we hadn't parted so badly. Or that it had been worse, so I could hate him.

I wish things were right with Hallie, but I won't be able to really fix them until I go home again. We've been best friends since our diaper days; I hope we'll work it out back in Woodbrock. That doesn't help me now, though.

I squinch my eyes shut and send Hallie a mental message, just like we agreed. *Call Ro. Call Ro. Call Ro.*

But, of course, she doesn't.

Mom asks me what I miss about being in Sydney. I try to tell her, but it's raspberry Jell-O again.

"I miss P-*people*," I say.

That isn't what I want to say, but it's all my mouth can manage.

Ro to Patrick. Ro to Patrick. Come in, Patrick Carroll.

The blue sky quivers with tears, but Patrick isn't there.

"Patrick." It comes as the tiniest whisper. Mom doesn't lift her head.

We hired a car today, and Mom's gone into a gallery. She's left her papers on the seat and they're kind of blowing about. Tasmania isn't as cold as Claire made out, but it's winter here, and where there's winter, there's wind.

I stack the papers, but one has gone down between the seats. I snag it between two fingers and put it on the stack.

John Smith. Background. Subject d.o.b., I read. Poor John Smith is the guy whose girlfriend was killed as they were going home from a date. No wonder he doesn't go to school. How do you ever get over a thing like that?

"You don't," says Patrick. "You learn to go around it."

"Say what?"

"What do you mean by that, Ro? I often wondered. Does it mean you didn't hear me, or is it just a way of buying time?"

I feel my face go stiff with surprise, and my scalp is kind of crawling. That *can't* be Patrick Carroll.

I close my eyes, then open them. And then I get out of the car. "Patrick?"

He's standing a little way off, with his hands stuffed in his pockets.

"Patrick?" I say again. "You jerk!" and I walk toward him on legs that feel like fettuccine.

I want to fall into his arms and have him kiss me. I

want to have him tell me he'll never let anything hurt me.

I don't do that, because it wouldn't help. The barrier between us is always going to be there. He won't let me into his life, and he won't come into mine.

"Oh, Patrick!" I say. He turns and looks at me, and his wounded eyes are more than I can stand. I reach out to touch his arm, but he flinches away. "What are you doing here?" I ask. "And *don't* say, 'Talking to you,' because you're not."

It must be the lump in my throat that makes me sound kind of snippy.

"I came to see you," he says. I see the shadow of his cute half smile lift the side of his mouth. "How have you been, Ro?"

"Lonesome," I say. I see something in his eyes, and hold up my hand. "Lonesome is no fun, but it's better than the wrong kind of company."

"And that means me?" he asks.

I lower myself onto the grass, and the chill strikes through my blue jeans. I put my arms around my knees, because I don't trust myself not to reach for him. I remember Tim's hand sliding under my shirt. I think I know how that happens. I want my hands on Patrick and my face against his cheek.

"You cleaned the shirt again," I said.

"I did?" He looks down at himself and pulls at the thick white cloth.

"Last time I saw you it was all messed up."

"I suppose that was after the bashing," he said.

I stare at him, and the back of my neck goes cold.

"I've decided to tell you," he says. "I've missed you so much, Ro, and he really does need a friend."

"*He?*" I say. Patrick has often puzzled me, but now he's not making sense.

"Yes, I am making sense," he says. "You just don't want to hear it."

I shiver, and it's not only because of the chill ground under my butt. I can't bear that he looks so unhappy, and he's right. I don't want to know what he's about to say.

"Can we go to Saint Valentine's Garden?" I ask.

He looks startled. "Aren't you afraid to go there with me? After the last time?"

"I'm not afraid of you," I say. "But Mom will be out here soon, and if you're going to tell me a story I don't want her bugging us."

"It won't take long," he says. "And I think it had better be here."

"OK," I say. I tuck my hands in my sweatshirt to keep them warm. "But you sit down." I take one hand out and pat the ground beside me, but Patrick sits a couple of feet away.

We look at each other. I don't know what's in my eyes, but Patrick's are so wide the black has almost swallowed the blue.

"Come on," I say at last. "What do you want to tell me?"

"It's hard to start," he says. He tries to give his cute smile, but it's nothing better than a jerk of his mouth. He knows it, too, because he suddenly puts his hands up over his face. I'm frightened for him now. It's as if he's falling apart in front of me.

"This isn't because of me," I say.

He shakes his head. "I should never have come to you," he says, "but it seemed such a chance to get a life. *He* was a mess, but I couldn't see why *I* shouldn't have someone. . . ."

"Patrick!" I say it firmly. I want him to snap out of this. "Say what you're going to say and stop jerking me around. Who's this *he?*"

Patrick takes his face out of his hands and stares at me. "Patrick Carroll, of course!"

"But *you're* Patrick Carroll."

"Not exactly," he says. He reaches for my hands and then shakes his head.

I scoot over to him. "Listen up," I say. "You recall when my head was hurting? You let me use you as a pillow. You're hurting now, so I'm paying it back. Don't read more into it than there is."

He gives me a startled look, and then does as I say. His face feels hot under my fingers, but the hard knot in my stomach begins to unravel. "So what's your name," I ask, stroking his forehead, "if it isn't Patrick Carroll?"

"I haven't really got one," he says. "Because I'm not really real."

"You lost me." I'm wishing Mom were here. She knows about people in trouble. "You feel real to me," I say, tracing my fingers over his cheek.

"I'm only a projection," says Patrick. "I'm the person he wants to be. He wants to be strong and healthy. He wants to have a girl and give her the stars and never let her be hurt. He wants it so badly he can taste it."

"But . . ."

He turns his cheek into my palm. "I have to say it all. I'm his other self. I'm the one he should have been, but I can do things he can't. He wants to get back into his life, but he doesn't know how. That's why he

183

invented me. He set me free to do all the things he couldn't. But he went a bit too far, so I can do things that other people can't."

The hair on the back of my neck is trying to stand up. My B-average brain is struggling to keep up. I'm no good at algebra. I don't understand how one thing can stand in as another.

"Ro," says the boy with his head in my lap, "you must have known I wasn't real. Walking in the clouds? Puh-*lease*."

"But you *are* real," I say. "You're as solid as me."

He smiles up at me, and it's almost his old smile. "You believe in me. So does he, of course, but there had to be someone else to believe in me too. There's nothing stronger than belief, Ro. You wanted me to be real, and so I am."

"But Mom and Hallie—"

"Your mother knows about him, not me," says Patrick. "She's got him in her papers. And she found out more from Tim Tilley."

I am struggling to understand, but my brain isn't happy about it.

"Never mind your brain," said Patrick. "Use the other thing. Imagination."

"Tell me if I've got this right," I say. "There's a boy called Patrick Carroll somewhere."

"Check!" he says, and lifts a thumb in the casual way Australians seem to have.

"Things went wrong in his life."

"Check."

"What things, exactly? He didn't kill anyone?"

"He used to feel as if he did, but he knows better

now." Patrick kisses my fingertips, and my stomach turns to water.

"Quit that!" I say.

"OK." He grins. "Keep your fingers away from my mouth."

Oops.

"He had a girl," says Patrick, "who used to get migraines. They were at a dance and she started to get the first signs. He tried to call her dad to come for her, but he'd had too much to drink and he said to catch a train. They started walking to the station. They walked right into a turf war. She was killed by accident, so the gang tried to keep him quiet. But he wasn't as dead as they thought."

"John Smith," I said. "The boy in Mom's case studies. But how does Tim Tilley come into it?"

"Tim is Pat's friend. He kept on going to see him, and he helped to get him back on track. He brings work from the college and stops in for a cup of coffee or a shake."

"Tim's a nice guy," I say.

"Yes," says Patrick, "but he's a bit of a spaz. He'll never get your name right."

"Petey?" I say. "Are you the one he calls Petey?"

Patrick groans.

"He calls me *Rena*. Does he know about *you?*"

"Hell, no!" says Patrick. "Tim's a good bloke, but doppelgangers aren't his thing."

I stare at him. "I don't know that they're my thing, either. What are they?"

Patrick's lips quiver and I can tell he's trying not to laugh. "A doppelganger is a double, Ro. It's German

185

for "double-goer"; a kind of ghostly twin that goes off and does the business you can't take care of yourself."

I'm not sure what I think about being "business" for a guy I've never met. "What about *him*?" I ask. "Your other self?"

"He's feeling better now," he says. "He doesn't have nightmares anymore. He's trying to put his life together and he's going to be OK. But he's still got a couple of problems."

"And I guess you're one of them?"

Patrick laughs. He really cracks me up, and I laugh too. "Now I know why I love you, Ro!" he says through a wave of chuckles. "Only you would come out with something like that."

"All right, already!" I say. I blot my eyes on my sleeve. "So what's his problem, *apart* from having you around the house?"

"He's not what you'd call an ordinary guy," says Patrick. "Before he got bashed up, he used to write songs and stories. He doesn't do that now, but all that creative stuff had to go somewhere."

"And I guess you're it?"

He nods. "He can't walk on clouds, or shift time and space, but he always imagined he could. And so I *can*. And he always wanted to kiss a girl in a garden of roses."

My head is spinning. Patrick still feels warm and solid, but I'm beginning to remember things. The shirt that never got wet, and a boy who went swimming in jeans.

"That's the way he pictured me, dressed in the outfit he was wearing when he went to that dance. Before it all went wrong."

"So you're not a little old hypnotist."

"No. But he is. He can't make you bark like a dog, or think you're a chair, but he uses self-hypnosis. Lots of artists do that. It's like tuning in to your inner self and using things you know already to create your own reality. Some people do it to give themselves confidence. Pat does it to explore his own world when the real one looks a bit too big and cold. And he's always had one hell of an imagination."

"Why *me*?" I ask. "Why did he pick on me?"

"He didn't," says Patrick. "I did. He'd projected me, and I looked down and saw you. You looked so out of place, and you didn't have a big social network already. That would have made it difficult to get your attention."

"You got my attention all right," I say. "Just three more things."

"Only *three*?"

"Why the Roach Hotel?"

"That's where he lives. He moved away from home to sort himself out. His flat isn't so bad. He's dead nuts on roaches."

"Why were you so frightened of letting me talk about you? Why the lip-zip?"

"If you'd blabbed about your boyfriend who took you swimming a thousand miles away, and walked you through the clouds, what do you think would have happened?"

"Mom would have had me in therapy until I'm ninety."

"Right," says Patrick softly. "You'd have had to talk to too many people. They'd all have disbelieved you, and then I'd be up in smoke. I *couldn't* let you expose me to all that disbelief. And then there's the other thing. He projected me in his image *before* the bashing. That means I don't remember much about the way he is now. If you ask me too many questions I don't have any matching memories, and then I start to doubt myself, and *pffft!*"

"But you're telling me now."

"Yes . . . I'm telling you now. I expect my time is nearly up, anyway. Soon he won't be needing me anymore."

I feel myself going cold. I thought he'd come to make up, and that maybe we could start again. Now I feel he has come to say good-bye.

"I'll never really be gone," says Patrick. "I think I'll just go back to where I began. But I had to come and tell you how sorry I am. I never meant to hurt you. I never thought things through."

"I can see why you had to keep me quiet," I say, "but couldn't you have explained? Couldn't you have trusted me to do the right thing? I trusted you, if you recall."

Patrick laughs again, but it isn't a very happy laugh. "I'm sorry, Ro, but if I'd explained, how could you have believed in me?"

"I'm believing in you now," I say stiffly.

"You've had a lot of practice now, but you were afraid at first. What's the third thing you wanted to ask?"

I look down at Patrick's face. I do not believe I'm hearing this. After all the things he wouldn't tell me before . . .

"I told you a lot," says Patrick. "You know about the pizza, and the dam, and the cracks. . . . I'm the water that comes out one way or another. You know the beautiful things that are terrible and the terrible things in beauty; the desert is alive and the roses can be dead. You know you can float in water if you only have the trick of it."

"Guess you're gonna tell me clouds are the same as water?"

"Well, they are. Just not so dense. Like me and him. He's the water. I'm the guy in the clouds."

"Why can't I ever remember how you look?" I blurt.

"Appearances don't matter. You loved me even when you didn't remember my face."

"You can't say things like that!" I yelp. "Guys *don't*."

"But I'm not your regular guy," he says. "I'm the way one guy would like to be." He looks wistfully up at me. "Do you still love me, now that you know what I am?"

"I'm thinking, I'm thinking . . ." I say. "How can I love someone who isn't quite real?"

Patrick laughs. "People do that all the time! It's part of human nature."

22

PAT.

So I'm sitting here in Tasmania, and a guy has his head in my lap. I'm waiting for Mom to come out, but I don't know what she'll see when she does.

"Mom would believe in you," I say. "She knows about John Smith. She might even know his name."

"She'd believe in me as a metaphorical symptomatic figment," says Patrick. "She'd believe so hard that pretty soon that's all I would be."

I sigh. "You're as bad as she is. What's *that* mean?"

"Think about it," says Patrick. "A metaphor is something described in terms of being something else, OK? Like 'a lake of shadow.' A symptom is an outward sign of something going on inside. Like a rash or a fever. A figment is an imaginary figure. Get it now?"

I think. I groan. "I guess so."

Patrick stares up at the sky. "Why didn't I ever try this pillow thing before?" he asks. "It's nice."

"You were too busy making like Man the Protector," I say. "I told you I don't need a hero."

The wind has dropped and I'm happy in the sun. I just don't want to think ahead.

"He wants to know if you'd like to meet him," says Patrick. He must see the shock in my face, because he smiles. "No pressure, Ro. He isn't looking for a girlfriend now. He just wants to meet someone who didn't know him before. He doesn't look the same, and sometimes people stare."

"Oh, Patrick!"

"Don't you meet him out of pity. He'd hate it."

"But what about Mom?"

Patrick laughs. "Your mother would *love* to get to meet a Smith in the flesh. Though really he's more of a Smith-Green."

"Mom says there's no such thing."

"What does she know? She only uses the concept . . . she doesn't own it. And he's really more Green than Smith right now. He knows it wasn't his fault."

"Are the Rockslides real?" I ask.

"Oh, yes," says Patrick. "All the places you went with me are real . . . except . . ."

"Saint Valentine's Garden," I say.

"Well . . . it's about as real as me." Patrick jumps up and leaves me feeling cold. "Like to pay it a visit for old times' sake?"

"*Yes!*" I say, and Patrick's smile lights up.

"Jump!" he says, and I jump and he catches me. And Saint Valentine's Garden is all around us.

It doesn't look the way it did when it was dying. It's green and quiet and full of dew and birds. It seems to be early morning, and early spring.

Patrick sets me down by the splashing fountain. "You ready, Ro?"

I nod.

"Then bring it on!" he says.

The buds all burst into flower, but it happens slowly. If I look at any bush I can see each blossom open. The sun comes out and the perfume rises around us. The roses are red and gold, crimson and pink and orange, and right in front of us they are blushing white.

Patrick holds out his arms to me and bends down to kiss me gently. "Love you, Ro," he says. And I look into his face and tell myself I must remember.

And then the garden fades and I'm back by the rented car.

Patrick is standing a few yards away with his hands stuffed into his pockets. He isn't looking at me. He's reading the sign outside the gallery.

"Wait up, Patrick!" I call.

My voice seems to startle him, and he makes a jerky movement with his shoulders.

I walk over the grass, kind of scuffing leaves with my sneakers.

"Patrick?" I put my hand on his arm, and he looks down at me.

But something isn't right. I stare at him in bewilderment, and he returns the stare with gray eyes. One side of his face is crossed with dull red scars, and when he moves I can tell one leg doesn't do quite what he wants.

I swallow. "Patrick?" I say again. I know I should let him go, but I go on holding his arm. It's thinner than I remember, and rigid with tension. Did he always look this way?

He smiles, kind of ruefully. "Hi. Do I know you?"

"My name's Rowena. I'm a friend of a friend of yours. You know Tim Tilley, don't you?"

"Good old Tim," he says. "Are you the girl he has the— Um. Sorry."

"He's a *buddy,*" I say firmly. "That's all. He knows my mom."

"I see." His voice is dry. "And he told you to come and be nice to poor old Petey, did he?"

"No." I feel sorry for him, but he's not getting away with that. "Listen up, Patrick Carroll . . . if that's who you are?"

"Well, I'm Pat to everyone but Tim. *Petey,* indeed."

"Listen up, Pat. I'm never nice to *anyone* because of being told. That would be kind of insulting."

"I wish everyone thought so," said Pat. "Why are you holding my arm? I'm not a cripple."

I feel a kind of bump in my stomach. It isn't the swoony feeling I used to get with Patrick, but it's a kind of exciting thing. This boy isn't a hero. He's got a prickly shell, but inside he's smart and funny. And he's always wanted to kiss a girl in a garden of roses. And somehow my Patrick Carroll is part of him.

"Well?" he says. "I limp a bit, but I don't need a human crutch, thanking you kindly."

"Well, guess what, jerk, I'm not about to be one!"

"So why are you still holding my arm?"

I look up at him and see the humor behind his eyes. He's enjoying this.

"Guess maybe I like the feel of it," I say. "Some girls like arms. Didn't you know? How do you come to be here, Pat? Don't you live in Sydney?"

He shrugs. "I came down last week on a cut-price tour. I'm supposed to be meeting someone, but they didn't show."

193

"That'd be me," I say. "And if you don't want Mom all over you, don't mention the words 'John Smith.' "

"Why would I?" He lifts one hand as if to touch my cheek, then snatches it back. "And why have you got rose petals in your hair?"

THE REAL DEAL

Unscripted
Amy Kaye

Thanks to the reality-TV show that records her junior year in excruciating detail, Claire Marangello gets her big break: her own version of the TV show and a starring role in a Broadway musical. Plus Jeb, a way-hot co-star who seems to like her *that* way, and a half sister she didn't know she had. It's everything she's ever dreamed of.

Or is it a total nightmare? Her sister seems to be drifting away. Claire's not sure she can trust Jeb and his weird celebrity-centered world. The director seems to hate her; the dance steps are harder than she'd ever imagined. Claire's about to learn that while being a Broadway star is a challenge, real life has twists and turns harder than any onstage choreography and is totally . . . *UNSCRIPTED*.

Amy Kaye

THE REAL DEAL
Focus on *THIS!*

Caught on tape: The newest reality television series goes on location somewhere truly dangerous—high school. Outrageous and unscripted, each episode exposes the sickest gossip, finds the facts behind the rumors, and bares the raw truth. Tune in and take it all in, because no subject is too taboo, no secret too private, and no behavior off limits!

Meet Fiona O'Hara—stuck in a suburban sitcom a million light-years away from her native New York City, a.k.a. civilization. Her mom is a basket case since the divorce. Her dad is Mr. Disappearo. And the one guy who seems like a decent love-interest has a psycho wannabe girlfriend who's ready to put a hit out on her.

CHLOE,
QUEEN OF DENIAL

NAOMI NASH

If you're reading this note, you're probably in the middle of the desert pulling it from the vulture-plucked bones of someone who used to be named Chloe Bryce.

Or maybe you're my poor, grieving parents who sent me to die in Egypt. A month at the Tomb of Tekhen and Tekhnet will look really good on your college resume, you said. Satisfied now, guys? Maybe you two didn't know I'd end up facing risks that would make Indiana Jones think twice—baths only every ten days, blistering heat, ancient tombs, mummies, a cursed bracelet . . . Of course, I did manage to kiss the dig's one hot guy—so you can console yourselves that I died somewhat happy!

EYELINER OF THE GODS
KATIE MAXWELL

To Whom It May Concern:

If you find this letter, it means that I, January James, have fallen down the burial shaft of the Tomb of Tekhen and Tekhnet where I'm spending a month working as a conservator, and am probably lying at the bottom, dead from a broken leg and thirst. . . .

To whoever finds my sand-scoured, withered corpse:

I'm dead. It's the mummy's curse. Don't blame Seth, he was just trying to help, even if everyone does say he's the reincarnation of an evil Egyptian god. He's not. I know, because no one who kisses like he does can be truly evil.

Help! I'm stuck in Egypt with a pushy girl named Chloe, a cursed bracelet, and a hottie who makes my toes curl. . . .

Got Fangs?

Confessions of a Vampire's Girlfriend

by Katie Maxwell

I used to think all I wanted was to have a normal life. You know, where I could be one of the crowd and blend in, so no one would know just how different I am. But now I'm stuck in the middle of Hungary with my mom, working for a traveling fair with psychics, magicians, and other really weird people, and somehow, blending in with this crowd doesn't look so good.

Fortunately, there's Benedikt. Yeah, he may be a vampire, but he has a motorcycle, he likes the mysterious horse I suddenly acquired, and best of all, he doesn't think I'm the least bit freaky. So I'm supposed to redeem his soul—if his kisses are anything to go by, my new life may not be quite as bad as I imagined.

Coming in January 2005!

Didn't want this book to end?

There's more waiting at **www.smoochya.com**:

Win FREE books and makeup!
Read excerpts from other books!
Chat with the authors!
Horoscopes!
Quizzes!
